Marx Joyce Abbott Hardy Machiavelli Montaigne Chesterton Cooper Emerson Austen Defoe Melville Haggard Hugo Eliot Grimm Stoker Carroll Christie Molière Wilde Maupassant Byron Schiller Garnett Einstein Fitzgerald Engels Smith Goethe Hawthorne Kafka Cotton Dostoyevsky Hall Baum Kipling Doyle Willis Leslie Dumas Henry Nietzsche Flaubert Turgenev Balzac Stockton Vatsyayana Crane Burroughs Verne Curtis Tocqueville Whitman Gogol Vinci Homer Widger Tolstoy Busch Darwin Thoreau Potter Freud Zola Twain Plato Scott Lawrence Kant Jowett Stevenson Dickens Andersen Burton Hesse Harte London Descartes Cervantes Poe Aristotle Wells Voltaire Hale James Hastings Cooke Bunner Shakespeare Richter Chambers Irving Chekhov da Shaw Wodehouse Benedict Doré Dante Swift Pushkin Alcott Newton tredition®

tredition was established in 2006 by Sandra Latusseck and Soenke Schulz. Based in Hamburg, Germany, tredition offers publishing solutions to authors and publishing houses, combined with worldwide distribution of printed and digital book content. tredition is uniquely positioned to enable authors and publishing houses to create books on their own terms and without conventional manufacturing risks.

For more information please visit: www.tredition.com

TREDITION CLASSICS

This book is part of the TREDITION CLASSICS series. The creators of this series are united by passion for literature and driven by the intention of making all public domain books available in printed format again - worldwide. Most TREDITION CLASSICS titles have been out of print and off the bookstore shelves for decades. At tredition we believe that a great book never goes out of style and that its value is eternal. Several mostly non-profit literature projects provide content to tredition. To support their good work, tredition donates a portion of the proceeds from each sold copy. As a reader of a TREDITION CLASSICS book, you support our mission to save many of the amazing works of world literature from oblivion. See all available books at www.tredition.com.

Project Gutenberg

The content for this book has been graciously provided by Project Gutenberg. Project Gutenberg is a non-profit organization founded by Michael Hart in 1971 at the University of Illinois. The mission of Project Gutenberg is simple: To encourage the creation and distribution of eBooks. Project Gutenberg is the first and largest collection of public domain eBooks.

Comic History of England

Bill Nye

Imprint

This book is part of TREDITION CLASSICS

Author: Bill Nye
Cover design: Buchgut, Berlin – Germany

Publisher: tredition GmbH, Hamburg - Germany
ISBN: 978-3-8424-4919-0

www.tredition.com
www.tredition.de

HEREIN WILL BE FOUND A RECITAL OF THE MANY EVENTFUL EVENTS WHICH TRANSPIRED IN ENGLAND FROM THE DRUIDS TO HENRY VIII. THE AUTHOR DOES NOT FEEL IT INCUMBENT ON HIM TO PRESERVE MORE THAN THE DATES AND FACTS, AND THESE ARE CORRECT, BUT THE LIGHTS AND SHADES OF THE VARIOUS PICTURES AND THE ORNAMENTAL WORDS FURNISHED TO ADORN THE CHARACTERS AND EVENTS ARE THE SOLE INVENTION OF THIS HISTORIAN.

1896

PREFACE.

The readers of this volume will share our regret that the preface cannot be written by Mr. Nye, who would have introduced his volume with a characteristically appropriate and humorous foreword in perfect harmony with the succeeding narrative.

We need only say that this work is in the author's best vein, and will prove not only amusing, but instructive as well; for the events, successions, dates, etc., are correct, and the trend of actual facts is adhered to. Of course, these facts are "embellished," as Mr. Nye would say, by his fancy, and the leading historical characters are made to play in fantastic *rôles*. Underneath all, however, a shrewd knowledge of human nature is betrayed, which unmasks motives and reveals the true inwardness of men and events with a humorous fidelity.

The unfortunate illness to which Mr. Nye finally succumbed prevented the completion of his history beyond the marriage of Henry VIII. to Anne Boleyn.

CHAPTER I.

INVASION OF CAESAR: THE DISCOVERY OF TIN AND CONSEQUENT ENLIGHTENMENT OF BRITAIN.

[Illustration: BUST OF CAESAR.]

From the glad whinny of the first unicorn down to the tip end of the nineteenth century, the history of Great Britain has been dear to her descendants in every land, 'neath every sky.

But to write a truthful and honest history of any country the historian should, that he may avoid overpraise and silly and mawkish sentiment, reside in a foreign country, or be so situated that he may put on a false moustache and get away as soon as the advance copies have been sent to the printers.

The writer of these pages, though of British descent, will, in what he may say, guard carefully against permitting that fact to swerve him for one swift moment from the right.

England even before Christ, as now, was a sort of money centre, and thither came the Phoenicians and the Carthaginians for their tin.

[Illustration: THE DISCOVERY OF TIN IN BRITAIN.]

[Illustration: CAESAR CROSSING THE CHANNEL.]

These early Britons were suitable only to act as ancestors. Aside from that, they had no good points. They dwelt in mud huts thatched with straw. They had no currency and no ventilation,—no drafts, in other words. Their boats were made of wicker-work plastered with clay. Their swords were made of tin alloyed with copper, and after a brief skirmish, the entire army had to fall back and straighten its blades.

They also had short spears made with a rawhide string attached, so that the deadly weapon could be jerked back again. To spear an enemy with one of these harpoons, and then, after playing him for half an hour or so, to land him and finish him up with a tin sword, constituted one of the most reliable boons peculiar to that strange people.

[Illustration: CAESAR TREATING WITH THE BRITONS.]

Caesar first came to Great Britain on account of a bilious attack. On the way across the channel a violent storm came up. The great emperor and pantata believed he was drowning, so that in an instant's time everything throughout his whole lifetime recurred to him as he went down,—especially his breakfast.

Purchasing a four-in-hand of docked unicorns, and much improved in health, he returned to Rome.

Agriculture had a pretty hard start among these people, and where now the glorious fields of splendid pale and billowy oatmeal may be seen interspersed with every kind of domestic and imported fertilizer in cunning little hillocks just bursting forth into fragrance by the roadside, then the vast island was a quaking swamp or covered by impervious forests of gigantic trees, up which with coarse and shameless glee would scamper the nobility.

(Excuse the rhythm into which I may now and then drop as the plot develops.—AUTHOR.)

Caesar later on made more invasions: one of them for the purpose of returning his team and flogging a Druid with whom he had disagreed religiously on a former trip. (He had also bought his team of the Druid.)

The Druids were the sheriffs, priests, judges, chiefs of police, plumbers, and justices of the peace.

[Illustration: PLOUGHING 51 B.C.]

They practically ran the place, and no one could be a Druid who could not pass a civil service examination.

[Illustration: DRUID SACRIFICES.]

They believed in human sacrifice, and often of a bright spring morning could have been seen going out behind the bush to sacrifice some one who disagreed with them on some religious point or other.

The Druids largely lived in the woods in summer and in debt during the winter. They worshipped almost everything that had been left out overnight, and their motto was, "Never do anything unless you feel like it very much indeed."

Caesar was a broad man from a religious point of view, and favored bringing the Druids before the grand jury. For uttering such sentiments as these the Druids declared his life to be forfeit, and set one of their number to settle also with him after morning services the question as to the matter of immersion and sound money.

Religious questions were even then as hotly discussed as in later times, and Caesar could not enjoy society very much for five or six days.

[Illustration: MONUMENT OF AGRICULTURE, OR ANCIENT SCARECROW.]

At Stonehenge there are still relics of a stone temple which the Druids used as a place of idolatrous worship and assassination. On Giblet Day people came for many miles to see the exercises and carry home a few cutlets of intimate friends.

After this Rome sent over various great Federal appointees to soften and refine the people. Among them came General Agricola with a new kind of seed-corn and kindness in his heart.

[Illustration: AGRICOLA ENCOURAGES AGRICULTURE.]

He taught the barefooted Briton to go out to the pump every evening and bathe his chapped and soil-kissed feet and wipe them on the grass before retiring, thus introducing one of the refinements of Rome in this cold and barbaric clime.

Along about the beginning of the Christian "Erie," says an elderly Englishman, the Queen Boadicea got so disgusted with the Romans who carried on there in England just as they had been in the habit of doing at home,—cutting up like a hallowe'en party in its junior year,—that she got her Britons together, had a steel dress made to fight in comfortably and not tight under the arms, then she said, "Is there any one here who hath a culverin with him?" One was soon found and fired. This by the Romans was regarded as an opening of hostilities. Her fire was returned with great eagerness, and victory was won in the city of London over the Romans, who had taunted the queen several times with being seven years behind the beginning of the Christian Era in the matter of clothes.

[Illustration: ROMAN COAT OF ARMS.]

Boadicea won victories by the score, and it is said that under the besom of her wrath seventy thousand Roman warriors kissed the dust. As she waved her sceptre in token of victory the hat-pin came out of her crown, and wildly throwing the "old hot thing" at the Roman general, she missed him and unhorsed her own chaperon.

Disgusted with war and the cooking they were having at the time, she burst into tears just on the eve of a general victory over the Romans and poisoned herself.

[Illustration: DEATH OF BOADICEA.]

N.B.—Many thanks are due to the author, Mr. A. Barber, for the use of his works entitled "Half-Hours with Crowned Heads" and "Thoughts on Shaving Dead People on Whom One Has Never Called," cloth, gilt top.

I notice an error in the artist's work which will be apparent to any one of moderate intelligence, and especially to the Englishman,—viz., that the tin discovered by the Phoenicians is in the form of cans, etc., formerly having contained tinned meats, fruits, etc. This book, I fear, will be sharply criticised in England if any inaccuracy be permitted to creep in, even through the illustrations. It is disagreeable to fall out thus early with one's artist, but the writer knows too well, and the sting yet burns and rankles in his soul where pierced the poisoned dart of an English clergyman two years ago. The writer had spoken of Julius Caesar's invasion of Britain for the purpose of replenishing the Roman stock of umbrellas, top-coats, and "loydies," when the clergyman said, politely but very firmly, "that England then had no top-coats or umbrellas." The writer would not have cared, had there not been others present.

CHAPTER II.

THE VARIOUS ROMAN YOKES: THEIR GROWTH, DEGENERATION, AND FINAL ELIMINATION.

Agricola no doubt made the Roman yoke easier upon the necks of the conquered people, and suggested the rotation of crops. He also invaded Caledonia and captured quite a number of Scotchmen, whom he took home and domesticated.

Afterwards, in 121 A.D., the emperor Hadrian was compelled to build a wall to keep out the still unconquered Caledonians. This is called the "Picts' Wall," and a portion of it still exists. Later, in 208 A.D., Severus built a solid wall of stone along this line, and for seventy years there was peace between the two nations.

Towards the end of the third century Carausius, who was appointed to the thankless task of destroying the Saxon pirates, shook off his allegiance to the emperor Diocletian, joined the pirates and turned out Diocletian, usurping the business management of Britain for some years. But, alas! he was soon assassinated by one of his own officers before he could call for help, and the assassin succeeded him. In those days assassination and inauguration seemed to go hand-in-hand.

[Illustration: ASSASSINATION OF CARAUSIUS.]

After Constantius, who died 306 A.D., came Constantine the Great, his son by a British princess.

Under Constantine peace again reigned, but the Irish, who desired to free Ireland even if they had to go abroad and neglect their business for that purpose, used to invade Constantine's territory, getting him up at all hours of the night and demanding that he should free Ireland.

These men were then called Picts, hence the expression "picked men."

They annoyed Constantine by coming over and trying to introduce Home
Rule into the home of the total stranger.

The Scots also made turbulent times by harassing Constantine and seeking to introduce their ultra-religious belief at the muzzle of the crossgun.

Trouble now came in the latter part of the fourth century A.D., caused by the return of the regular Roman army, which went back to Rome to defend the Imperial City from the Goths who sought to "stable their stock in the palace of the Caesars," as the historian so tersely puts it.

[Illustration: THE PICTS INCULCATING HOME RULE PRINCIPLES.]

In 418 A.D., the Roman forces came up to London for the summer, and repelled the Scots and Picts, but soon returned to Rome, leaving the provincial people of London with disdain. Many of the Roman officers while in Britain had their clothes made in Rome, and some even had their linen returned every thirty days and washed in the Tiber.

[Illustration: IRRITABILITY OF THE BARBARIAN.]

In 446 A.D., the Britons were extremely unhappy. "The barbarians throw us into the sea and the sea returns us to the barbarians," they ejaculated in their petition to the conquering Romans. But the latter were too busy fighting the Huns to send troops, and in desperation the Britons formed an alliance with Hengist and Horsa, two Saxon travelling men who, in 449 A.D., landed on the island of Thanet, and thus ended the Roman dominion over Britain.

[Illustration: LANDING OF HENGIST AND HORSA.]

The Saxons were at that time a coarse people. They did not allow etiquette to interfere with their methods of taking refreshment, and, though it pains the historian at all times to speak unkindly of his ancestors who have now passed on to their reward, he is compelled to admit that as a people the Saxons may be truly characterized as a great National Appetite.

During the palmy days when Rome superintended the collecting of customs and regulated the formation of corporations, the mining and smelting of iron were extensively carried on and the "walking delegate" was invented. The accompanying illustration shows an ancient strike.

[Illustration: DISCOMFORTS OF THE EARLY LABOR AGITATOR.]

Rome no doubt did much for England, for at that time the Imperial City had 384 streets, 56,567 palaces, 80 golden statues, 2785 bronze statues of former emperors and officers, 41 theatres, 2291 prisons, and 2300 perfumery stores. She was in the full flood of her prosperity, and had about 4,000,000 inhabitants.

In those days a Roman Senator could not live on less than $80,000 per year, and Marcus Antonius, who owed $1,500,000 on his inaugural, March 15, paid it up March 17, and afterwards cleared $720,000,000. This he did by the strictest economy, which he managed to have attended to by the peasantry.

Even a literary man in Rome could amass property, and Seneca died worth $12,000,000. Those were the flush times in Rome, and England no doubt was greatly benefited thereby; but, alas! "money matters became scarce," and the poor Briton was forced to associate with the delirium tremens and massive digestion of the Saxon, who floated in a vast ocean of lard and wassail during his waking hours and slept with the cunning little piglets at night. His earthen floors were carpeted with straw and frescoed with bones.

Let us not swell with pride as we refer to our ancestors, whose lives were marked by an eternal combat between malignant alcoholism and trichinosis. Many a Saxon would have filled a drunkard's grave, but wabbled so in his gait that he walked past it and missed it.

[Illustration: THE SAXON IDEA OF HEAVEN.]

To drink from the skulls of their dead enemies was a part of their religion, and there were no heretics among them.[A]

[Footnote A: The artist has very ably shown here a devoted little band of Saxons holding services in a basement. In referring to it as "abasement," not the slightest idea of casting contumely or obloquy on our ancestors is intended by the humble writer of pungent but sometimes unpalatable truth.]

Christianity was introduced into Britain during the second century, and later under Diocletian the Christians were greatly persecuted. Christianity did not come from Rome, it is said, but from Gaul. Among the martyrs in those early days was St. Alban, who had been converted by a fugitive priest. The story of his life and death is familiar.

The Bible had been translated, and in 314 A.D. Britain had three Bishops, viz., of London, Lincoln, and York.

CHAPTER III.

THE ADVENT OF THE ANGLES: CAUSES WHICH LED TO THE REHABILITATION OF BRITAIN ON NEW LINES.

With the landing of Hengist and Horsa English history really begins, for Caesar's capture of the British Isles was of slight importance viewed in the light of fast-receding centuries. There is little to-day in the English character to remind one of Caesar, who was a volatile and epileptic emperor with massive and complicated features.

The rich warm blood of the Roman does not mantle in the cheek of the Englishman of the present century to any marked degree. The Englishman, aping the reserve and hauteur of Boston, Massachusetts, is, in fact, the diametrical antipode of the impulsive, warm-hearted, and garlic-imbued Roman who revels in assassination and gold ear-bobs.

The beautiful daughter of Hengist formed an alliance with Vortigern, the royal foreman of Great Britain,—a plain man who was very popular in the alcoholic set and generally subject to violent lucid intervals which lasted until after breakfast; but the Saxons broke these up, it is said, and Rowena encouraged him in his efforts to become his own worst enemy, and after two or three patent-pails-full of wassail would get him to give her another county or two, until soon the Briton saw that the Saxon had a mortgage on the throne, and after it was too late, he said that immigration should have been restricted.

[Illustration: ROWENA CAPTIVATES VORTIGERN.]

Kent became the first Saxon kingdom, and remained a powerful state for over a century.

More Saxons now came, and brought with them yet other Saxons with yet more children, dogs, vodka, and thirst. The breath of a

Saxon in a cucumber-patch would make a peck of pickles per moment.

The Angles now came also and registered at the leading hotels. They were destined to introduce the hyphen on English soil, and plant the orchards on whose ancestral branches should ultimately hang the Anglo-Saxon race, the progenitors of the eminent aristocracy of America.

Let the haughty, purse-proud American—in whose warm life current one may trace the unmistakable strains of bichloride of gold and trichinae—pause for one moment to gaze at the coarse features and bloodshot eyes of his ancestors, who sat up at nights drenching their souls in a style of nepenthe that it is said would remove moths, tan, freckles, and political disabilities.

[Illustration: ETHELBERT, KING OF KENT, PROCLAIMED "BRETWALDA."]

The seven states known as the Saxon Heptarchy were formed in the sixth
and seventh centuries, and the rulers of these states were called
"Bretwaldas," or Britain-wielders. Ethelbert, King of Kent, was
Bretwalda for fifty years, and liked it first-rate.

[Illustration: AUGUSTINE KINDLY RECEIVED BY ETHELBERT, KING OF KENT.]

A very good picture is given here showing the coronation of Ethelbert, copied from an old tin-type now in the possession of an aged and somewhat childish family in Philadelphia who descended from Ethelbert and have made no effort to conceal it.

Here also the artist has shown us a graphic picture of Ethelbert supported by his celebrated ingrowing moustache receiving Augustine. They both seem pleased to form each other's acquaintance, and the greeting is a specially appetizing one to the true lover of Art for Art's sake.

For over one hundred and fifty years the British made a stubborn resistance to the encroachments of these coarse people, but it was ineffectual. Their prowess, along with a massive appetite and other hand baggage, soon overran the land of Albion. Everywhere the rude warriors of northern Europe wiped the dressing from their coarse red whiskers on the snowy table-cloth of the Briton.

[Illustration: THEY WIPED THEIR COARSE RED WHISKERS ON THE SNOWY
TABLE-CLOTH.]

In West Wales, or Dumnonia, was the home of King Arthur, so justly celebrated in song and story. Arthur was more interesting to the poet than the historian, and probably as a champion of human rights and a higher civilization should stand in that great galaxy occupied by Santa Claus and Jack the Giant-Killer.

The Danes or Jutes joined the Angles also at this time, and with the Saxons spread terror, anarchy, and common drunks all over Albion. Those who still claim that the Angles were right Angles are certainly ignorant of English history. They were obtuse Angles, and when bedtime came and they tried to walk a crack, the historian, in a spirit of mischief, exclaims that they were mostly a pack of Isosceles Try Angles, but this doubtless is mere badinage.

They were all savages, and their religion was entirely unfit for publication. Socially they were coarse and repulsive. Slaves did the housework, and serfs each morning changed the straw bedding of the lord and drove the pigs out of the boudoir. The pig was the great social middle class between the serf and the nobility: for the serf slept with the pig by day, and the pig slept with the nobility at night.

And yet they were courageous to a degree (the Saxons, not the pigs). They were fearless navigators and reckless warriors. Armed with their rude meat-axes and one or two Excalibars, they would take something in the way of a tonic and march right up to the mouth of the great Thomas catapult, or fall in the moat with a courage that knew not, recked not of danger.

Christianity was first preached in Great Britain in 597 A.D., at the suggestion of Gregory, afterwards Pope, who by chance saw some Anglican youths exposed for sale in Rome. They were fine-looking fellows, and the good man pitied their benighted land. Thus the

Roman religion was introduced into England, and was first to turn the savage heart towards God.

[Illustration: EGBERT GAINS A GREAT VICTORY OVER THE FRENCH INVADERS.]

Augustine was very kindly received by Ethelbert, and invited up to the house. Augustine met with great success, for the king experienced religion and was baptized, after which many of his subjects repented and accepted salvation on learning that it was free. As many as ten thousand in one day were converted, and Augustine was made Archbishop of Canterbury. On a small island in the Thames he built a church dedicated to St. Peter, where now is Westminster Abbey, a prosperous sanctuary entirely out of debt.

The history of the Heptarchy is one of murder, arson, rapine, assault and battery, breach of the peace, petty larceny, and the embezzlement of the enemy's wife.

In 827, Egbert, King of Wessex and Duke of Shandygaff, conquered all his foes and became absolute ruler of England (Land of the Angles). Taking charge of this angular kingdom, he established thus the mighty country which now rules the world in some respects, and which is so greatly improved socially since those days.

Two distinguished scholars flourished in the eighth century, Bede and Alcuin. They at once attracted attention by being able to read coarse print at sight. Bede wrote the Ecclesiastical History of the Angles. It is out of print now. Alcuin was a native of York, and with the aid of a lump of chalk and the side of a vacant barn could figure up things and add like everything. Students flocked to him from all over the country, and matriculated by the dozen. If he took a fancy to a student, he would take him away privately and show him how to read.

The first literary man of note was a monk of Whitby named Caedmon, who wrote poems on biblical subjects when he did not have to monk. His works were greatly like those of Milton, and especially like "Paradise Lost," it is said.

Gildas was the first historian of Britain, and the scathing remarks made about his fellow-countrymen have never been approached by the most merciless of modern historians.

The book was highly interesting, and it is a wonder that some enterprising American publisher has not appropriated it, as the author is now extremely dead.

[Illustration: A DISCIPLE OF THE LIQUID RELIGION PRACTISED BY THE
SAXON.]

CHAPTER IV.

THE INFLUX OF THE DANES: FACTS SHOWING CONCLUSIVELY THEIR INFLUENCE ON THE BRITON OF TO-DAY.

And now, having led the eager student up to the year 827 A.D., let us take him forward from the foundation of the English monarchy to the days of William the Conqueror, 1066.

Egbert, one of the kings of Wessex, reigned practically over Roman Britain when the country was invaded by the Northmen (Swedes, Norwegians, and Danes), who treated the Anglo-Saxon as the Anglo-Saxon had formerly treated the poor Briton.

These Northmen were rather coarse people, and even put the Anglo-Saxons to the blush sometimes. They exercised vigorously, and thus their appetites were sharp enough to cut a hair. They at first came in the capacity of pirates,—sliding stealthily into isolated coast settlements on Saturday evening and eating up the Sunday victuals, capturing the girls of the Bible-class and sailing away. But later they came as conquerors, and boarded with the peasantry permanently.

Egbert formed an alliance with his old enemies, the Welsh, and gained a great victory over the Northmen; but when he died and left Ethelwolf, his son, in charge of the throne, he made a great mistake. Ethelwolf was a poor king, "being given more to religious exercises than reigning," says the historian. He would often exhibit his piety in order to draw attention away from His Royal Incompetency. He was not the first or last to smother the call to duty under the cry of Hallelujah. Like the little steamer engine with the big whistle, when he whistled the boat stopped. He did not have a boiler big enough to push the great ship of state and shout Amen at the same time.

Ethelwolf defeated the enemy in one great battle, but too late to prevent a hold-up upon the island of Thanet, and afterwards at Shippey, near London, where the enemy settled himself.

Yet Ethelwolf made a pilgrimage to Rome with Alfred, then six years old (A.D. 855). He was gone a year, during which time very little reigning was done at home, and the Northmen kept making treaties and coming over in larger droves.

Ethelwolf visited Charles the Bald of France at this time, and married his daughter Judith incidentally. Ethelwolf's eldest son died during the king's absence, and was succeeded as eldest son by Ethelbald (heir-apparent, though he had no hair apparent), who did not recognize the old gentleman or allow him to be seated on his own throne when he came back; but Ethelwolf gave the naughty Ethelbald the western half of the kingdom rather than have trouble. But Baldy died, and was succeeded by Ethelbert, who died six years later, and Ethelred, in 866, took charge till 871, when he died of a wound received in battle and closed out the Ethel business to Alfred.

The Danes had meantime rifled the country with their cross-guns and killed Edmund, the good king of East Anglia, who was afterwards canonized, though gunpowder had not then been invented.

Alfred was not only a godly king, but had a good education, and was a great admirer of Dickens and Thackeray. (This is put in as a titbit for the critic.)

He preferred literature to the plaudits of the nobility and the sedentary life on a big white-oak throne. On the night before his coronation his pillow was wet with tears.

And in the midst of it all here came the Danes wearing heavy woollen clothes and introducing their justly celebrated style of honest sweat.

Alfred fought as many as eight battles with them in one year. They agreed at last to accept such portions of the country as were assigned them, but they were never known to abide by any treaty, and they put the red man of America to shame as prevaricators.

Thus, by 878, the wretched Saxons were at their wit's end, and have never been able to take a joke since at less than thirty days.

Some fled to Wales and perished miserably trying to pronounce the names of their new post-office addresses.

[Illustration: ALFRED, DISGUISED AS A GLEEMAN, IS INTRO-DUCED TO
GUTHRUN.]

Here Alfred's true greatness stood him in good stead. He secured a number of reliable retainers and camped in the swamps of Somersetshire, where he made his head-quarters on account of its inaccessibility, and then he made raids on the Danes. Of course he had to live roughly, and must deny himself his upright piano for his country's good.

In order to obtain a more thorough knowledge of the Danes and their number, he disguised himself as a harper, or portable orchestra, and visited the Danish camp, where he was introduced to Guthrun and was invited to a banquet, where he told several new anecdotes, and spoke in such a humorous way that the army was sorry to see him go away, and still sorrier when, a few days later, armed *cap-a-pie,* he mopped up the greensward with his enemy and secured the best of terms from him.

While *incog.,* Alfred stopped at a hut, where he was asked to turn the pancakes as they required it; but in the absence of the hostess he got to thinking of esoteric subjects, or something profound, and allowed the cakes to burn. The housewife returned in time to express her sentiments and a large box to his address as shown in the picture.

[Illustration: ALFRED LETTING THE CAKES BURN.]

He now converted Guthrun and had him immersed, which took first-rate, and other Danes got immersed. Thus the national antagonism to water was overcome, and to-day the English who are descended from the Danes are not appalled at the sight of water.

As a result of Guthrun's conversion, the Danes agreed to a permanent settlement along the exposed portion of Great Britain, by which they became unconsciously a living rampart between the Saxons and other incursionists.

Now peace began to reign up to 893, and Alfred improved the time by rebuilding the desolated cities,—London especially, which had become a sight to behold. A new stock-law, requiring the peasantry to shut up their unicorns during certain seasons of the year and keep them out of the crops, also protecting them from sportsmen while shedding their horns in spring, or moulting, it is said, was passed, but the English historians are such great jokers that the writer has had much difficulty in culling the facts and eliminating the persiflage from these writings.

Alfred the Great only survived his last victory over the Danes, at Kent, a few years, when he died greatly lamented. He was a brave soldier, a successful all-around monarch, and a progressive citizen in an age of beastly ignorance, crime, superstition, self-indulgence, and pathetic stupidity.

[Illustration: ALFRED ESTABLISHED SCHOOLS.]

He translated several books for the people, established or repaired the University of Oxford, and originated the idea, adopted by the Japanese a thousand years later, of borrowing the scholars of other nations, and cheerfully adopting the improvements of other countries, instead of following the hide-bound and stupid conservatism and ignorance bequeathed by father to son, as a result of blind and offensive pride, which is sometimes called patriotism.

[Illustration: KING ALFRED TRANSLATED SEVERAL BOOKS.]

CHAPTER V.

THE TROUBLOUS MIDDLE AGES: DEMONSTRATING A SHORT REIGN FOR THOSE WHO TRAVEL AT A ROYAL GAIT.

The Ethels now made an effort to regain the throne from Edward the Elder. Ethelwold, a nephew of Edward, united the Danes under his own banner, and relations were strained between the leaders until 905, when Ethelwold was slain. Even then the restless Danes and frontier settlers were a source of annoyance until about 925, when Edward died; but at his death he was the undisputed king of all Britain, and all the various sub-monarchs and associate rulers gave up their claims to him. He was assisted in his affairs of state by his widowed sister, Ethelfleda. Edward the Elder had his father's ability as a ruler, but was not so great as a scholar or *littérateur*. He had not the unfaltering devotion to study nor the earnest methods which made Alfred great. Alfred not only divided up his time into eight-hour shifts,—one for rest, meals, and recreation, one for the affairs of state, and one for study and devotion,—but he invented the candle with a scale on it as a time-piece, and many a subject came to the throne at regular periods to set his candle by the royal lights.

[Illustration: CAME TO THE THRONE AT REGULAR PERIODS
TO SET THEIR
CANDLES BY THE ROYAL LIGHT.]

Think of those days when the Sergeant-at-Arms of Congress could not turn back the clock in order to assist an appropriation at the close of the session, but when the light went out the session closed.

Athelstan succeeded his father, Edward the Presiding Elder, and resembled him a good deal by defeating the Welsh, Scots, and Danes. In those days agriculture, trade, and manufacturing were diversions during the summer months; but the regular business of life was warfare with the Danes, Scots, and Welsh.

These foes of England could live easily for years on oatmeal, sour milk, and cod's heads, while the fighting clothes of a whole regiment would have been a scant wardrobe for the Greek Slave, and after two centuries of almost uninterrupted carnage their war debt was only a trifle over eight dollars.

Edmund, the brother of Ethelstan, at the age of eighteen, succeeded his brother on the throne.

One evening, while a little hilarity was going on in the royal apartments, Edmund noticed among the guests a robber named Leolf, who had not been invited. Probably he was a pickpocket; and as a royal robber hated anybody who dropped below grand larceny, the king ordered his retainers to put him out.

But the retainers shrank from the undertaking, therefore Edmund sprang from the throne like a tiger and buried his talons in the robber's tresses. There was a mixture of feet, legs, teeth, and features for a moment, and when peace was restored King Edmund had a watch-pocket full of blood, and the robber chieftain was wiping his stabber on one of the royal tidies.

[Illustration: EDMUND THROWING LEOLF OUT.]

Edred now succeeded the deceased Edmund, his brother, and with a heavy heart took up the eternal job of fighting the Danes. Edred set up a sort of provincial government over Northumberland, the refractory district, and sent a governor and garrison there to see that the Danes paid attention to what he said. St. Dunstan had considerable influence over Edred, and was promoted a great deal by the king, who died in the year 955.

He was succeeded by Edwy the Fair, who was opposed by another Ethel. Between the Ethels and the Welsh and Danes, there was little time left in England for golf or high tea, and Edwy's reign was short and full of trouble.

He had trouble with St. Dunstan, charging him with the embezzlement of church funds, and compelled him to leave the country. This was in retaliation for St. Dunstan's overbearing order to the king. One evening, when a banquet was given him in honor of his coronation, the king excused himself when the speeches got rather corky, and went into the sitting-room to have a chat with his wife, Elgiva, of whom he was very fond, and her mother. St. Dunstan, who had still to make a speech on Foreign Missions with a yard or so of statistics, insisted on Edwy's return. An open outbreak was the result. The Church fell upon the King with a loud, annual report, and when the débris was cleared away, a little round-shouldered grave in the churchyard held all that was mortal of the king. His wife was cruelly and fatally assassinated, and Edgar, his brother, began to reign. This was in the year 959, and in what is now called the Middle Ages.

Edgar was called the Pacific. He paid off the church debt, made Dunstan Archbishop of Canterbury, helped reform the church, and, though but sixteen years of age when he removed all explosives from the throne and seated himself there, he showed that he had a massive scope, and his subjects looked forward to much anticipation.

He sailed around the island every year to show the Danes how prosperous he was, and made speeches which displayed his education.

His coronation took place thirteen years after his accession to the throne, owing to the fact, as given out by some of the more modern historians, that the crown was at Mr. Isaac Inestein's all this time, whereas the throne, which was bought on the instalment plan, had been redeemed.

Pictures of the crown worn by Edgar will convince the reader that its redemption was no slight task, while the mortgage on the throne was a mere bagatelle.

[Illustration: EDGAR SURMOUNTED BY HIS CROWN.]

[Illustration: EDGAR CAUSES HIS BARGE TO BE ROWED BY EIGHT KINGS.]

A bright idea of Edgar's was to ride in a row-boat pulled by eight kings under the old *régime*.

Personally, Edgar was reputed to be exceedingly licentious; but the historian wisely says these stories may have been the invention of his enemies. Greatness is certain to make of itself a target for the mud of its own generation, and no one who rose above the level of his surroundings ever failed to receive the fragrant attentions of those who had not succeeded in rising. All history is fraught also with the bitterness and jealousy of the historian except this one. No bitterness can creep into this history.

Edgar, it is said, assassinated the husband of Elfrida in order that he might marry her. It is also said that he broke into a convent and carried off a nun; but doubtless if these stories were traced to their very foundations, politics would account for them both.

He did not favor the secular clergy, and they, of course, disliked him accordingly. He suffered also at the hands of those who sought to operate the reigning apparatus whilst his attention was turned towards other matters.

He was the author of the scheme whereby he utilized his enemies, the Welsh princes, by demanding three hundred wolf heads per annum as tribute instead of money. This wiped out the wolves and used up the surplus animosity of the Welsh.

As the Welsh princes had no money, the scheme was a good one. Edgar died at the age of thirty-two, and was succeeded by Edward, his son, in 975.

The death of the king at this early age has given to many historians the idea that he was a sad dog, and that he sat up late of nights and cut up like everything, but this may not be true. Death often takes the good, the true, and the beautiful whilst young.

However, Edgar's reign was a brilliant one for an Anglo-Saxon, and his coon-skin cap is said to have cost over a pound sterling.

[Illustration: EDGAR THE PACIFIC.]

CHAPTER VI.

THE DANISH OLIGARCHY: DISAFFECTIONS ATTENDING CHRONIC USURPATION PROCLIVITIES.

Edgar was succeeded by his son Edward, called "the Martyr," who ascended the throne at the age of fifteen years. His step-mother, Elfrida, opposed him, and favored her own son, Ethelred. Edward was assassinated in 978, at the instigation of his step-mother, and that's what's the martyr with him.

During his reign there was a good deal of ill feeling, and Edward would no doubt have been deposed but for the influence of the church under Dunstan.

Ethelred was but ten years old when he began reigning. Sadly poor Dunstan crowned him, his own eyes still wet with sorrow over the cruel death of Edward. He foretold that Ethelred would have a stormy reign, with sleet and variable winds, changing to snow.

During the remainder of the great prelate's life he, as it were, stood between the usurper and the people, and protected them from the threatening storm.

But in 991, shortly after the death of Dunstan, a great army of Norwegians came over to England for purposes of pillage. To say that it was an allopathic pillage would not be an extravagant statement. They were extremely rude people, like all the nations of northern Europe at that time,—Rome being the Boston of the Old World, and Copenhagen the Fort Dodge of that period.

The Norwegians ate everything that did not belong to the mineral kingdom, and left the green fields of merry England looking like a base-ball ground. So wicked and warlike were they that the sad and defeated country was obliged to give the conquering Norske ten thousand pounds of silver.

Dunstan died at the age of sixty-three, and years afterwards was canonized; but firearms had not been invented at the time of his death. He led the civilization and progress of England, and was a pioneer in cherishing the fine arts.

Olaf, who led the Norwegians against England, afterwards became king of Norway, and with the Danes used to ever and anon sack Great Britain,—*i.e.*, eat everybody out of house and home, and then ask for a sack of silver as the price of peace.

Ethelred was a cowardly king, who liked to wear the implements of war on holidays, and learn to crochet and tat in time of war. He gave these invaders ten thousand pounds of silver at the first, sixteen thousand at the second, and twenty-four thousand on the third trip, in order to buy peace.

Olaf afterwards, however, embraced Christianity and gave up fighting as a business, leaving the ring entirely to Sweyn, his former partner from Denmark, who continued to do business as before.

The historian says that the invasion of England by the Norwegians and Danes was fully equal to the assassination, arson, and rapine of the Indians of North America. A king who would permit such cruel cuttings-up as these wicked animals were guilty of on the fair face of old England, should live in history only as an invertebrate, a royal failure, a decayed mollusk, and the dropsical head of a tottering dynasty.

In order to strengthen his feeble forces, Ethelred allied himself, in 1001, to Richard II., Duke of Normandy, and married his daughter Emma, but the Danes continued to make night hideous and elope with ladies whom they had never met before. It was a sad time in the history of England, and poor Emma wept many a hot and bitter tear as she yielded one jewel after another to the pawnbroker in order to buy off the coarse and hateful Danes.

If Ethelred were to know how he is regarded by the historian who pens these lines, he would kick the foot-board out of his casket, and bite himself severely in four places.

To add to his foul history, happening to have a few inoffensive Danes on hand, on the 13th of November, the festival of St. Brice, 1002, he gave it out that he would massacre these people, among them the sister of the Danish king, a noble woman who had become a Christian (only it is to be hoped a better one), and married an English earl. He had them all butchered.

[Illustration: ETHELRED WEDS EMMA.]

In 1003, Sweyn, with revenge in his heart, began a war of extermination or subjugation, and never yielded till he was, in fact, king of England, while the royal intellectual polyp, known as Ethelred the Unwholesome, fled to Normandy, in the 1013th year Anno Domini.

But in less than six weeks the Danish king died, leaving the sceptre, with the price-mark still upon it, to Canute, his son, and Ethelred was invited back, with an understanding that he should not abuse his privileges as king, and that, although it was a life job during good behavior, the privilege of beheading him from time to time was and is vested in the people; and even to-day there is not a crowned head on the continent of Europe that does not recognize this great truth,—viz., that God alone, speaking through the united voices of the common people, declares the rulings of the Supreme Court of the Universe.

On the old autograph albums of the world is still written in the dark corners of empires, "*the king can do no wrong*." But where education is not repressed, and where that Christianity which is built on love and charity is taught, there can be but one King who does no wrong.

Ethelred was succeeded by Edmund, called "the Ironside." He fought bravely, and drove the Danes, under Canute, back to their own shores. But they got restless in Denmark, where there was very little going on, and returned to England in large numbers.

Ethelred died in London, 1016 A.D., before Canute reached him. He was called by Dunstan "Ethelred the Unready," and had a faculty for erring more promptly than any previous king.

Having returned cheerily from Ethelred's rather tardy funeral, the people took oath, some of them under Edmund and some under Canute.

Edmund, after five pitched battles, offered to stay bloodshed by personally fighting Canute at any place where they could avoid police interference, but Canute declined, on what grounds it is not stated, though possibly on the Polo grounds.

[Illustration: SONS OF EDMUND SENT TO OLAF.]

A compromise was agreed to in 1016, by which Edmund reigned over the region south of the Thames; but very shortly afterwards he was murdered at the instigation of Edric, a traitor, who was the Judas Iscariot of his time.

Canute, or "Knut," now became the first Danish king of England. Having appointed three sub-kings, and taken charge himself of Wessex, Canute sent the two sons of Edmund to Olaf, requesting him to put them to death; but Olaf, the king of Sweden, had scruples, and instead of doing so sent the boys to Hungary, where they were educated. Edward afterwards married a daughter of the Emperor Henry II.

Canute as king was, after he got the hang of it, a great success, giving to the harassed people more comfort than they had experienced since the death of Alfred, who was thoroughly gifted as a sovereign.

He had to raise heavy taxes in order to 'squire himself with the Danish leaders at first, but finally began to harmonize the warring elements, and prosperity followed. He was fond of old ballads, and encouraged the wandering minstrels, who entertained the king with topical songs till a late hour. Symposiums and after-dinner speaking were thus inaugurated, and another era of good feeling began about half-past eleven o'clock each evening.

[Illustration: THE SEA "GOES BACK" ON CANUTE.]

Queen Emma, the widow of Ethelred, now began to set her cap for Canute, and thus it happened that her sons again became the heirs to the throne at her marriage, A.D. 1017.

Canute now became a good king. He built churches and monasteries, and even went on a pilgrimage to Rome, which in those days was almost certain to win public endorsement.

Disgusted with the flattering of his courtiers, one day as he strolled along the shore he caused his chair to be placed at the margin of the approaching tide, and as the water crept up into his lap, he showed them how weak must be a mortal king in the presence of Omnipotence. He was a humble and righteous king, and proved by his example that after all the greatest of earthly rulers is only the most obedient servant.

He was even then the sovereign of England, Norway, and Denmark. In 1031 he had some trouble with Malcolm, King of Scotland, but subdued him promptly, and died in 1035, leaving Hardicanute, the son of Emma, and Sweyn and Harold, his sons by a former wife.

Harold succeeded to the English throne, Sweyn to that of Norway, and
Hardicanute to the throne of Denmark.

In the following chapter a few well-chosen remarks will be made regarding Harold and other kings.

CHAPTER VII.

OTHER DISAGREEABLE CLAIMANTS: FOREIGN FOIBLES INTRODUCED, ONLY TO BE EXPUNGED WITH CHARACTERISTIC PUGNACITY.

Let us now look for a moment into the reigns of Harold I. and Hardicanute, a pair of unpopular reigns, which, although brief, were yet long enough.

Queen Emma, of course, desired the coronation of Hardicanute, but, though supported by Earl Godwin, a man of great influence and educated to a high degree for his time, able indeed, it is said, at a moment's notice, to add up things and reduce things to a common denominator, it could not be.

Harold, the compromise candidate, reigned from 1037 to 1040. He gained Godwin to his side, and together they lured the sons of Emma by Ethelred—viz., Alfred and Edward—to town, and, as a sort of royal practical joke, put out Alfred's eyes, causing his death.

Harold was a swift sprinter, and was called "Harefoot" by those who were intimate enough to exchange calls and coarse anecdotes with him.

He died in 1040 A.D., and nobody ever had a more general approval for doing so than Harold.

Hardicanute now came forth from his apartments, and was received as king with every demonstration of joy, and for some weeks he and dyspepsia had it all their own way on Piccadilly. (Report says that he drank! Several times while under the influence of liquor he abdicated the throne with a dull thud, but was reinstated by the Police.)

[Illustration: "KING HAROLD IS DEAD, SIRE."]

Enraged by the death of Alfred, the king had the remains of Harold exhumed and thrown into a fen. This a-fensive act showed what a great big broad nature Hardicanute had,—also the kind of timber used in making a king in those days.

Godwin, however, seems to have been a good political acrobat, and was on more sides of more questions than anybody else of those times. Though connected with the White-Cap affair by which Alfred lost his eyesight and his life, he proved an alibi, or spasmodic paresis, or something, and, having stood a compurgation and "ordeal" trial, was released. The historian very truly but inelegantly says, if memory serves the writer accurately, that Godwin was such a political straddle-bug that he early abandoned the use of pantaloons and returned to the toga, which was the only garment able to stand the strain of his political cuttings-up.

The *Shire Mote*, or county court of those days, was composed of a dozen thanes, or cheap nobles, who had to swear that they had not read the papers, and had not formed or expressed an opinion, and that their minds were in a state of complete vacancy. It was a sort of primary jury, and each could point with pride to the vast collection he had made of things he did not know, and had not formed or expressed an opinion about.

[Illustration: "ORDEAL" OF JUSTICE.]

If one did not like the verdict of this court, he could appeal to the king on a *certiorari* or some such thing as that. The accused could clear himself by his own oath and that of others, but without these he had to stand what was called the "ordeal," which consisted in walking on hot ploughshares without expressing a derogatory opinion regarding the ploughshares or showing contempt of court. Sometimes the accused had to run his arm into boiling water. If after three days the injury had disappeared, the defendant was discharged and costs taxed against the king.

[Illustration: DYING BETWEEN COURSES.]

Hardicanute only reigned two years, and in 1042 A.D. died at a nuptial banquet, and cast a gloom over the whole thing. In those times it was a common thing for the king or some of the nobility to die between the roast pig and the pork pie. It was not unusual to see each noble with a roast pig *tête-à-tête,*—each confronting the other, the living and the dead.

At this time, it is said by the old settlers that hog cholera thinned out the nobility a good deal, whether directly or indirectly they do not say.

The English had now wearied of the Danish yoke. "Why wear the Danish yoke," they asked, "and be ruled with a rod of iron?"

Edward, half brother of Edmund Ironside, was therefore nominated and chosen king. Godwin, who seemed to be specially gifted as a versatile connoisseur of "crow,"[A] turned up as his political adviser.

[Footnote A: "Eating crow" is an expression common in modern American politics to signify a reluctant acknowledgement of humiliating defeat—HISTORIAN.]

Edward, afterwards called "the Confessor," at once stripped Queen Emma of all her means, for he had no love left for her, as she had failed repeatedly to assist him when he was an outcast, and afterwards the new king placed her in jail (or gaol, rather) at Winchester. This should teach mothers to be more obedient, or they will surely come to some bad end.

Edward was educated in Normandy, and so was quite partial to the Normans. He appointed many of them to important positions in both church and state. Even the See of Canterbury was given to a Norman. The See saw how it was going, no doubt, and accepted the position. But let us pass on rapidly to something else, for thereby variety may be given to these pages, and as one fact seems to call for another, truth, which for the time being may be apparently crushed to earth, may rise again.

[Illustration: EDWARD STRIPS EMMA OF HER MEANS.]

Godwin disliked the introduction of the Norman tongue and Norman customs in England, and when Eustace, Count of Boulogne and author of the sausage which bears his name, committed an act of violence against the people of Dover, they arose as one man, drove out the foreigners, and fumigated the town as well as the ferry running to Calais.

This caused trouble between Edward and Godwin, which led to the deposition of the latter, who, with his sons, was compelled to flee. But later he returned, and his popularity in England among the home people compelled the king to reëstablish him.

[Illustration: GODWIN AND HIS SONS FLYING FROM ENGLAND.]

Soon afterwards Godwin died, and Harold, his son, succeeded him successfully. Godwin was an able man, and got several earldoms for his wife and relatives at a time when that was just what they needed. An earldom then was not a mere empty title with nothing in it but a blue sash and a scorbutic temperament, but it gave almost absolute authority over one or more shires, and was also a good piece of property. These historical facts took place in or about the year 1054 A.D.

Edward having no children, together with a sort of misgiving about ever having any to speak of, called home Edward "the Outlaw," son of Edmund Ironside, to succeed to the throne; but scarcely had he reached the shores of England when he died, leaving a son, Edgar.

William of Normandy, a cousin of the king, now appears on the scene. He claimed to be entitled to the first crack at the throne, and that the king had promised to bequeath it to him. He even lured Harold, the heir apparently, to Normandy, and while under the influence of stimulants compelled Harold to swear that he would sustain William's claim to the throne. The wily William also inserted some holy relics of great potency under the altar used for swearing purposes, but Harold recovered when he got out again into the fresh air, and snapped his fingers at William and his relics.

[Illustration: WILLIAM COMPELLING HAROLD TO SWEAR.]

January 5, 1066, Edward died, and was buried in Westminster Abbey, which had just been enclosed and the roof put on.

Harold, who had practised a little while as earl, and so felt that he could reign easily by beginning moderately and only reigning forenoons, ascended the throne.

Edward the Confessor was a good, durable monarch, but not brilliant. He was the first to let people touch him on Tuesdays and Fridays for scrofula, or "king's evil." He also made a set of laws that were an improvement on some of the old ones. He was canonized about a century after his death by the Pope, but as to whether it "took" or not the historian seems strangely dumb.

[Illustration: WILLIAM OF NORMANDY LEARNS THAT HAROLD IS ELECTED KING.]

He was the last of the royal Saxon line; but other self-made Saxons reigned after him in torrents.

Edgar Atheling, son of Edward the Outlaw, was the only surviving male of the royal line, but he was not old enough to succeed to the throne, and Harold II. accepted the portfolio. He was crowned at Westminster on the day of King Edward's burial. This infuriated William of Normandy, who reminded Harold of his first-degree oath, and his pledge that he would keep it "or have his salary cut from year to year."

Oh, how irritated William was! He got down his gun, and bade the other
Normans who desired an outing to do the same.

Trouble also arose with Tostig, the king's brother, and his Norwegian ally, Hardrada, but the king defeated the allied forces at Stamford Bridge, near York, where both of these misguided leaders bit the dust. Previous to the battle there was a brief parley, and the king told Tostig the best he could do with him. "And what can you give my ally, Hardrada?" queried the astute Tostig. "Seven feet of English ground," answered the king, roguishly, "or possibly more, as Hardrada is rather taller than the average," or words to that effect. "Then let the fight go on," answered Tostig, taking a couple of hard-boiled eggs from his pocket and cracking them on the pommel of his saddle, for he had not eaten anything but a broiled shote since breakfast.

That night both he and Hardrada occupied a double grave on the right-hand side of the road leading to York.

CHAPTER VIII.

THE NORMAN CONQUEST: COMPLEX COMMINGLING OF FACETIOUS ACCORD AND IMPLACABLE DISCORD.

[Illustration: WILLIAM THE CONQUEROR.]

The Norman invasion was one of the most unpleasant features of this period. Harold had violated his oath to William, and many of his superstitious followers feared to assist him on that account. His brother advised him to wait a few years and permit the invader to die of exposure. Thus, excommunicated by the Pope and not feeling very well anyway, Harold went into the battle of Hastings, October 14, 1066. For nine hours they fought, the English using their celebrated squirt-guns filled with hot water and other fixed ammunition. Finally Harold, while straightening his sword across his knee, got an arrow in the eye, and abandoned the fight in order to investigate the surprises of a future state.

In this battle the contusions alone amounted to over ninety-seven, to say nothing of fractures, concussions, and abrasions.

Among other casualties, the nobility of the South of England was killed.

Harold's body was buried by the sea-shore, but many years afterwards disinterred, and, all signs of vitality having disappeared, he was buried again in the church he had founded at Waltham.

The Anglo-Saxons thus yielded to the Normans the government of England.

In these days the common people were called churls, or anything else that happened to occur to the irritable and quick-witted nobility. The rich lived in great magnificence, with rushes on the floor, which were changed every few weeks. Beautiful tapestry—similar to the rag-carpet of America—adorned the walls and prevented ventilation.

Glass had been successfully made in France and introduced into England.
A pane of glass indicated the abode of wealth, and a churl cleaning the
window with alcohol by breathing heavily upon it, was a sign that Sir
Reginald de Pamp, the pampered child of fortune, dwelt there.

To twang the lyre from time to time, or knock a few mellow plunks out of the harp, was regarded with much favor by the Anglo-Saxons, who were much given to feasting and merriment. In those pioneer times the "small and early" had not yet been introduced, but "the drunk and disorderly" was regarded with much favor.

Free coinage was now discussed, and mints established. Wool was the principal export, and fine cloths were taken in exchange from the Continent. Women spun for their own households, and the term spinster was introduced.

The monasteries carefully concealed everything in the way of education, and even the nobility could not have stood a civil service examination.

The clergy were skilled in music, painting, and sculpture, and loved to paint on china, or do sign-work and carriage painting for the nobility. St. Dunstan was quite an artist, and painted portraits which even now remind one strangely of human beings.

[Illustration: ST. DUNSTAN WAS NOTED FOR THIS KIND OF THING.]

Edgar Atheling, the legal successor of Harold, saw at a glance that William the Conqueror had come to stay, and so he yielded to the Norman, as shown in the accompanying steel engraving copied from a piece of tapestry now in possession of the author, and which descended to him, through no fault of his own, from the Normans, who for years ruled England with great skill, and from whose loins he sprang.

[Illustration: EDGAR ATHELING AND THE NOBILITY OFFER SUBMISSION TO

WILLIAM THE CONQUEROR.]

William was crowned on Christmas Day at Westminster Abbey as the new sovereign. It was more difficult to change a sovereign in those days than at present, but that is neither here nor there.

The people were so glad over the coronation that they overdid it, and their ghoulish glee alarmed the regular Norman army, the impression getting out that the Anglo-Saxons were rebellious, when as a matter of fact they were merely exhilarated, having tanked too often with the tankard.

William the Conqueror now disarmed the city of London, and tipping a number of the nobles, got them to wait on him. He rewarded his Norman followers, however, with the contraband estates of the conquered, and thus kept up his conking for years after peace had been declared.

But the people did not forget that they were there first, and so, while William was in Normandy, in the year 1067 A.D., hostilities broke out. People who had been foreclosed and ejected from their lands united to shoot the Norman usurper, and it was not uncommon for a Norman, while busy usurping, to receive an arrow in some vital place, and have to give up sedentary pursuits, perhaps, for weeks afterwards.

[Illustration: SAXONS INTRODUCING THE YOKE IN SCOTLAND.]

In 1068 A.D., Edgar Atheling, Sweyn of Denmark, Malcolm of Scotland, and the sons of Harold banded together to drive out the Norman. Malcolm was a brave man, and had, it is said, captured so many Anglo-Saxons and brought them back to Scotland, that they had a very refining influence on that country, introducing the study of the yoke among other things with moderate success.

[Illustration: WILLIAM WAS FOND OF HUNTING.]

William hastily returned from Normandy, and made short work of the rebellion. The following year another outbreak occurring in Northumberland, William mischievously laid waste sixty miles of fertile country, and wilfully slaughtered one hundred thousand people,—men, women, and children. And yet we have among us those who point with pride to their Norman lineage when they ought to be at work supporting their families.

In 1070 the Archbishop of Canterbury was degraded from his position, and a Milanese monk on his Milan knees succeeded him. The Saxons became serfs, and the Normans used the school tax to build large, repulsive castles in which to woo the handcuffed Anglo-Saxon maiden at their leisure. An Anglo-Saxon maiden without a rope ladder in the pocket of her basque was a rare sight. Many very thrilling stories are written of those days, and bring a good price.

William was passionately fond of hunting, and the penalty for killing a deer or boar without authority was greater than for killing a human being out of season.

In order to erect a new forest, he devastated thirty miles of farming country, and drove the people, homeless and foodless, to the swamps. He also introduced the curfew, which he had rung in the evening for his subjects in order to remind them that it was time to put out the lights, as well as the cat, and retire. This badge of servitude caused great annoyance among the people, who often wished to sit up and visit, or pass the tankard about and bid dull care begone.

William, however, was not entirely happy. While reigning, his children grew up without proper training. Robert, his son, unhorsed the old gentleman at one time, and would have killed him anonymously, each wearing at the time a galvanized iron dinner-pail over his features, but just at the fatal moment Robert heard his father's well-known breath asserting itself, and withheld his hand.

William's death was one of the most attractive features of his reign. It resulted from an injury received during an invasion of France.

Philip, the king of that country, had said something derogatory regarding William, so the latter, having business in France, decided to take his army with him and give his soldiers an outing. William captured the city of Mantes, and laid it in ashes at his feet. These ashes were still hot in places when the great conqueror rode through them, and his horse becoming restive, threw His Royal

Altitoodleum on the pommel of his saddle, by reason of which he received a mortal hurt, and a few weeks later he died, filled with remorse and other stimulants, regretting his past life in such unmeasured terms that he could be heard all over the place.

[Illustration: DEMISE OF WILLIAM THE CONQUEROR.]

The "feudal system" was now fully established in England, and lands descended from father to son, and were divided up among the dependants on condition of the performance of vassalage. In this way the common people were cheerily permitted the use of what atmosphere they needed for breathing purposes, on their solemn promise to return it, and at the close of life, if they had succeeded in winning the royal favor, they might contribute with their humble remains to the fertility of the royal vegetable garden.

[Illustration: THE FEUDAL SYSTEM WAS NOW FULLY ESTABLISHED.]

CHAPTER IX.

THE FEUDAL SYSTEM: SUCCESSFUL INAUGURATION OF HOMOGENEAL METHODS FOR RESTRICTING INCOMPATIBLE DEMAGOGUES.

At this time, under the reign of William, a year previous to his death, an inventory was taken of the real estate and personal property contained in the several counties of England; and this "Domesday-book," as it was called, formed the basis for subsequent taxation, etc. There were then three hundred thousand families in England. The book had a limited circulation, owing to the fact that it was made by hand; but in 1783 it was printed.

William II., surnamed "Rufus the Red," the auburn-haired son of the king, took possession of everything—especially the treasure—before his father was fully deceased, and by fair promises solidified the left wing of the royal party, compelling the disaffected Norman barons to fly to France.

William II. and Robert his brother came to blows over a small rebellion organized by the latter, but Robert yielded at last, and joined William with a view to making it hot for Henry, who, being a younger brother, objected to wearing the king's cast-off reigning clothes. He was at last forced to submit, however, and the three brothers gayly attacked Malcolm, the Scotch malecontent, who was compelled to yield, and thus Cumberland became English ground. This was in 1091.

[Illustration: WILLIAM II. TAKES POSSESSION OF THE ROYAL TRUNK AND
SECURES THE CROWN.]

In 1096 the Crusade was creating much talk, and Robert, who had expressed a desire to lead a totally different life, determined to go if money could be raised. Therefore William proceeded to levy on everything that could be realized upon, such as gold and silver communion services and other bric-à-brac, and free coinage was then first inaugurated. The king became so greedy that on the death of the Archbishop of Canterbury he made himself *ex-officio* archbishop, so that he might handle the offerings and coin the plate. When William was ill he sent for Father Anselm, but when he got well he took back all his sweet promises, in every way reminding one of the justly celebrated policy pursued by His Sulphureous Highness the Devil.

The capture of Jerusalem by the Crusaders very naturally attracted the attention of other ambitious princes who wished also to capture it, and William, Prince of Guienne, mortgaged his principality to England that he might raise money to do this; but when about to embark for the purpose of taking possession of this property, William II., the royal note-shaver, while hunting, was shot accidentally by a companion, or assassinated, it is not yet known which, and when found by a passing charcoal-burner was in a dead state. He was buried in 1100, at Winchester.

[Illustration: RUFUS FOUND DEAD IN THE FOREST BY A POOR CHARCOAL-BURNER.]

Rufus had no trouble in securing the public approval of his death. He was the third of his race to perish in the New Forest, the scene of the Conqueror's cruelty to his people. He was a thick-set man with a red face, a debauchee of the deepest dye, mean in money matters, and as full of rum and mendacity as Sitting Bull, the former Regent of the Sioux Nation. He died at the age of forty-three years, having reigned and cut up in a shameful manner for thirteen years.

Robert having gone to the Holy Land, Henry I. was crowned at Westminster. He was educated to a higher degree than William, and knew the multiplication table up to seven times seven, but he was highly immoral, and an armed chaperon stood between him and common decency.

He also made rapid strides as a liar, and even his own grocer would not trust him. He successfully fainted when he heard of his son's death, 1120 A.D.

His reign closed in 1135, when Stephen, a grandson of the Conqueror, with the aid of a shoe-horn assumed the crown of England, and, placing a large damp towel in it, proceeded to reign. He began at once to swap patronage for kind words, and every noble was as ignoble as a phenomenal thirst and unbridled lust could make him. Every farm had a stone jail on it, in charge of a noble jailer. Feudal castles, full of malaria and surrounded by insanitary moats and poor plumbing, echoed the cry of the captive and the bacchanalian song of the noble. The country was made desolate by duly authorized robbers, who, under the Crusaders' standard, prevented the maturity of the spring chicken and hushed the still, small voice of the roast pig in death.

[Illustration: HENRY FAINTED WHEN HE HEARD THE SAD NEWS.]

William the Conqueror was not only remembered bitterly in the broken hearts of his people, but in history his name will stand out forever because of his strange and grotesque designs on posterity.

In 1141 Stephen was made prisoner, and for five years he was not restored to his kingdom. In the mean time, Matilda, the widow of Henry I., encouraged by the prelates, landed in England to lay claim to the throne, and after a great deal of ill feeling and much needed assassination, her son Henry, who had become quite a large property-owner in France, invaded England, and finally succeeded in obtaining recognition as the rightful successor of Stephen. Stephen died in 1153, and Henry became king.

[Illustration: MATILDA LANDING IN ENGLAND.]

The Feudal System, which obtained in England for four hundred years, was a good one for military purposes, for the king on short notice might raise an army by calling on the barons, who levied on their vassals, and they in turn levied on their dependants.

A feudal castle was generally built in the Norman style of architecture. It had a "donjon," or keep, which was generally occupied by the baron as a bar-room, feed-trough, and cooler between fights. It was built of stone, and was lighted by means of crevices through the wall by day, and by means of a saucer of tallow and a string or rush which burned during the night and served mainly to show

how dark it was. There was a front yard or fighting-place around this, surrounded by a high wall, and this again by a moat. There was an inner court back of the castle, into which the baron could go for thinking. A chapel was connected with the institution, and this was the place to which he retired for the purpose of putting arnica on his conscience.

Underneath the castle was a large dungeon, where people who differed with the baron had a studio. Sometimes they did not get out at all, but died there in their sins, while the baron had all the light of gospel and chapel privileges up-stairs.

The historian says that at that time the most numerous class in England were the "villains." This need not surprise us, when we remember that it was as much as a man's life was worth to be anything else.

There were also twenty-five thousand serfs. A serf was required to be at hand night or day when the baron needed some one to kick. He was generally attached to the realty, like a hornet's nest, but not necessary to it.

In the following chapter knighthood and the early hardware trade will be touched upon.

[Illustration: "IN HOC SIGNO VINCES."]

CHAPTER X.

THE AGE OF CHIVALRY: LIGHT DISSERTATION ON THE KNIGHTS-ERRANT, MAIDS, FOOLS, PRELATES, AND OTHER NOTORIOUS CHARACTERS OF THAT PERIOD.

The age of chivalry, which yielded such good material to the poet and romancer, was no doubt essential to the growth of civilization, but it must have been an unhappy period for legitimate business. How could trade, commerce, or even the professions, arts, or sciences, flourish while the entire population spread itself over the bleaching-boards, day after day, to watch the process of "jousting," while the corn was "in the grass," and everybody's notes went to protest?

Then came the days of knight-errantry, when parties in malleable-iron clothing and shirts of mail—which were worn without change—rode up and down the country seeking for maids in distress. A pretty maid in those days who lived on the main road could put on her riding-habit, go to the window up-stairs, shed a tear, wave her kerchief in the air, and in half an hour have the front lawn full of knights-errant tramping over the peony beds and castor-oil plants.

[Illustration: A PRETTY MAID IN THOSE DAYS.]

In this way a new rescuer from day to day during the "errant" season might be expected. Scarcely would the fair maid reach her destination and get her wraps hung up, when a rattle of gravel on the window would attract her attention, and outside she would see, with swelling heart, another knight-errant, who crooked his Russia-iron elbow and murmured, "Miss, may I have the pleasure of this escape with you?"

"But I do not recognize you, sir," she would straightway make reply; and well she might, for, with his steel-shod countenance and corrugated-iron clothes, he was generally so thoroughly *incog.* that his crest, on a new shield freshly painted and grained and bearing a motto, was his only introduction. Imagine a sweet girl, who for years had been under the eagle eye of a middle-weight chaperon, suddenly espying in the moonlight a disguised man under the window on horseback, in the act of asking her to join him for a few weeks at his shooting-box in the swamp. Then, if you please, imagine her asking for his card, whereupon he exposes the side of his new tin shield, on which is painted in large Old English letters a Latin motto meaning, "It is the early bird that catches the worm," with bird rampant, worm couchant on a field uncultivated.

Then, seating herself behind the knight, she must escape for days, and even weeks,—one escape seeming to call for another, as it were. Thus, however, the expense of a wedding was saved, and the knight with the biggest chest measurement generally got the heiress with the copper-colored hair.

[Illustration: CREST OF A POPULAR KNIGHT.]

He wore a crest on his helmet adorned with German favors given him by lady admirers, so that the crest of a popular young knight often looked like a slump at the *Bon Marché*.

[Illustration: THE "VIGIL OF ARMS."]

The most peculiar condition required for entry into knighthood was the "vigil of arms," which consisted in keeping a long silent watch in some gloomy spot—a haunted one preferred—over the arms he was about to assume. The illustration representing this subject is without doubt one of the best of the kind extant, and even in the present age of the gold-cure is suggestive of a night-errant of to-day.

A tournament was a sort of refined equestrian prize-fight with one-hundred-ounce jabbers. Each knight, clad in tin-foil and armed cap-a-pie, riding in each other's direction just as fast as possible with an uncontrollable desire to push one's adversary off his horse, which meant defeat, because no man could ever climb a horse in full armor without a feudal derrick to assist him.

[Illustration: A JUDICIAL COMBAT.]

The victor was entitled to the horse and armor of the vanquished, which made the castle paddock of a successful knight resemble the convalescent ward of the Old Horses' Home.

This tourney also constituted the prevailing court of those times, and the plaintiff, calling upon God to defend the right, charged upon the defendant with a charge which took away the breath of his adversary. This, of course, was only applicable to certain cases, and could not be used in trials for divorce, breach of promise, etc.

The tournament was practically the forerunner of the duel. In each case the parties in effect turned the matter over to Omnipotence; but still the man who had his back to the sun, and knew how to handle firearms and cutlery, generally felt most comfortable.

Gentlemen who were not engaged in combat, but who attended to the grocery business during the Norman period, wore a short velvet cloak trimmed with fur over a doublet and hose. The shoes were pointed,—as were the remarks made by the irate parent,—and generally the shoes and remarks accompanied each other when a young tradesman sought the hand of the daughter, whilst she had looked forward to a two-hundred-mile ride on the crupper of a knight-errant without stopping for feed or water.

In those days also, the fool made no effort to disguise his folly by going to Congress or fussing with the currency, but wore a uniform which designated his calling and saved time in estimating his value.

The clergy in those days possessed the bulk of knowledge, and had matters so continued the vacant pew would have less of a hold on people than it has to-day; but in some way knowledge escaped from the cloister and percolated through the other professions, so that to-day in England, out of a good-sized family, the pulpit generally has to take what is left after the army, navy, politics, law, and golf have had the pick. It was a fatal error to permit the escape of knowledge in that way; and when southern Europe, now priest-ridden and pauperized, learns to read and write, the sleek blood-suckers will eat plainer food and the poor will not go entirely destitute.

The Normans ate two meals a day, and introduced better cooking among the Saxons, who had been accustomed to eat very little except while under the influence of stimulants, and who therefore did not realize what they ate. The Normans went in more for meat victuals, and thus the names of meat, such as veal, beef, pork, and mutton, are of Norman origin, while the names of the animals in a live state are calf, ox, pig, and sheep, all Saxon names.

The Authors' Club of England at this time consisted of Geoffrey of Monmouth and another man. They wrote their books with quill pens, and if the authorities did not like what was said, the author could be made to suppress the entire edition for a week's board, or for a bumper of Rhenish wine with a touch of pepper-sauce in it he would change the objectionable part by means of an eraser.

[Illustration: THE AUTHORS' CLUB AT THIS TIME.]

It was under these circumstances that the Plantagenets became leaders in society, and added their valuable real estate in France to the English dominions. In 1154, Henry Plantagenet was thus the most powerful monarch in Europe, and by wedding his son Geoffrey to the daughter of the Duke of Brittany, soon scooped in that valuable property also.

He broke up the custom of issuing pickpocket and felony licenses to his nobles, seized the royal stone-piles and other nests for common sneak thieves, and resolved to give the people a chance to pay taxes and die natural deaths. The disorderly nobles were reduced to the ranks or sent away to institutions for inebriates, and people began to permit their daughters to go about the place unarmed.

Foreign mercenaries who had so long infested the country were ordered to leave it under penalty of having their personal possessions confiscated, and their own carcasses dissected and fed to the wild boars.

[Illustration: FOREIGN MERCENARIES LEAVE ENGLAND.]

Henry next gave his attention to the ecclesiastic power. He chose Thomas à Becket to the vacant portfolio as Archbishop of Canterbury, hoping thus to secure him as an ally; but à Becket, though accustomed to ride after a four-in-hand and assume a style equal to the king himself, suddenly became extremely devout, and austerity characterized this child of fortune, insomuch that each day on bended knees he bathed the chapped and soiled feet of thirteen beggars. Why thirteen beggars should come around every morning to the archbishop's study to have their feet manicured, or how that could possibly mollify an outraged God, the historian does not claim to state, and, in fact, is not able to throw any light upon it at the price agreed upon for this book.

[Illustration: A COOLNESS BETWEEN THE KING AND THE ARCHBISHOP.]

Trouble now arose between the king and the archbishop; a protracted coolness, during which the king's pew grew gray with dust, and he had to baptize and confirm his own children in addition to his other work.

The king now summoned the prelates; but they excused themselves from coming on the grounds of previous engagements. Then he summoned the nobles also, and gave the prelates one more chance, which they decided to avail themselves of. Thus the "Constitutions of Clarendon" were adopted in 1164, and Becket, though he at first bolted the action of the convention, soon became reconciled and promised to fall into line, though he hated it like sin.

Then the Roman pontiff annulled the constitutions, and scared Becket back again into his original position. This angered the king, who condemned his old archbishop, and he fled to France, where he had a tall time. The Pope threatened to excommunicate Henry; but the latter told him to go ahead, as he did not fear excommunication, having been already twice exposed to it while young.

Finally à Becket was banished; but after six years returned, and all seemed again smooth and joyous; but Becket kept up the war indirectly against Henry, till one day he exclaimed in his wrath, "Is there no one of my subjects who will rid me of this insolent priest?" Whereupon four loyal knights, who were doubtless of Scotch extraction, and who therefore could not take a joke, thought the king in dead earnest, and actually butchered the misguided archbishop in a sickening manner before the altar. This was in 1170.

Henry, who was in France when this occurred, was thoroughly horrified and frightened, no doubt. So much so, in fact, that he agreed to make a pilgrimage barefoot to the tomb of à Becket; but even this did not place him upon a firm footing with the clergy, who paraded à Becket's assassination on all occasions, and thus strengthened this opposition to the king.

[Illustration: HENRY WALKING TO THE TOMB OF BECKET.]

CHAPTER XI.

CONQUEST OF IRELAND: UNCOMFORTABLE EFFECTS FOLLOWING THE CULTIVATION OF AN ACQUISITORIAL PROPENSITY.

In 1173 occurred the conquest of Ireland, anciently called Hibernia. These people were similar to the Britons, but of their history prior to the year 400 A.D. little is known. Before Christ a race of men inhabited Ireland, however, who had their own literature, and who were advanced in the arts. This was before the introduction of the "early mass" whiskers, and prior to the days when the Orangemen had sent forth their defiant peal.

[Illustration: "EARLY MASS" WHISKERS.]

In the fifth century Ireland was converted by St. Patrick, and she became known as the Island of Saints and Scholars. To say that she has become the island of pugilists and policemen to-day would be unjust, and to say that she has more influence in America than in Ireland would be unkind. Surely her modern history is most pathetic.

For three centuries the island was harassed by the Danes and Northmen; but when the Marquis of Queensberry rules were adopted, the latter threw up the sponge. The finish fight occurred at Clontarf, near Dublin.

Henry had written permission from the Pope to conquer Ireland years and years before he cared to do it. Sometimes it rained, and at other times he did not feel like it, so that his permission got almost worn out by carrying it about with him.

In 1172, however, an Irish chief, or subordinate king, had trouble with his kingdom,—doubtless because some rival monarch stepped in it and tracked it around over the other kingdoms,—and so he called upon the Anglo-Normans under Strongbow (Richard de Clare), whose deClaration of Independence was the first thing of the kind known to civilization, for help. While assisting the Irish chief, Strongbow noticed a royal wink on the features of Henry, and acting upon it proceeded to gather in the other precincts of Ireland. Thus, in 1172, the island was placed under the rule of a viceroy sent there by England.

Henry now had trouble with three of his sons, Henry, Richard, and Geoffrey, who threatened that if the old gentleman did not divide up his kingdom among them they would go to Paris and go into the *roué* business. Henry himself was greatly talked about, and his name coupled with that of fair Rosamond Clifford, a rival of Queen Eleanor. The king refused to grant the request of his sons, and bade them go ahead with their *roué* enterprises so long as they did not enter into competition with him.

[Illustration: THE BECKET DIFFICULTY STILL KEPT HENRY AWAKE AT NIGHT.]

So they went to Paris, where their cuttings-up were not noticed. The queen took their side, as also did Louis of France and William, King of Scotland. With the Becket difficulty still keeping him awake of nights also, the king was in constant hot water, and for a time it seemed that he would have to seek other employment; but his masterly hit in making a barefooted pilgrimage to the tomb of Becket, thus securing absolution from the Archbishop of Canterbury, turned the tide.

William of Scotland was made a prisoner in 1174, and the confederacy against the king broken up. Thus, in 1175, the castle at Edinburgh came into the hands of the English, and roast beef was substituted for oats. Irish and Scotch whiskey were now introduced into the national policy, and bits of bright English humor, with footnotes for the use of the Scots, were shipped to Edinburgh.

Henry had more trouble with his sons, however, and they embittered his life as the sons of a too-frolicsome father are apt to do. Henry Jr. died repentant; but Geoffrey perished in his sins in a tournament, although generally the tournament was supposed to be conducive to longevity. Richard was constitutionally a rebel, and at last compelled the old gentleman to yield to a humiliating treaty with the French in 1189. Finding in the list of the opposing forces the name of John, his young favorite son, the poor old battered monarch, in 1189, selected an unoccupied grave and took possession of same.

[Illustration: THE UNHAPPY FATHER SANK INTO THE GRAVE.]

He cursed his sons and died miserably, deserted by his followers, who took such clothing as fitted them best, and would have pawned the throne had it not been out of style and unavailable for that purpose, beside being secured to the castle. His official life was creditable to a high degree, but his private life seemed to call loudly for a good, competent disinfectant.

[Illustration: WHEN RICHARD WAS SICK THE GENEROUS SULTAN SENT HIM FRUITS
AND ICE.]

Richard *Kyur duh le ong*, as the French have it, or Richard I. of the lion heart, reigned in his father's stead from 1189 to 1199. His reign opened with a disagreeable massacre. The Jews, who had brought him some presents to wear at his inaugural ball, were insulted by the populace, who believed that the king favored a massacre, and so many were put to death.

Richard and Philip of France organized a successful crusade against people who were not deemed orthodox, and succeeded in bagging a good many in Syria, where the woods were full of infidels.

Richard, however, was so overbearing that Philip could not get along with him, and they dissolved partnership; but Richard captured Ascalon after this. His army was too much reduced, however, to capture Jerusalem.

Saladin, the opposing sultan, was a great admirer of Richard, and when the lion-hearted king was ill, sent him fruits and even ice, so the historian says. Where the Saracens got their ice at that time we can only surmise.

Peace was established, and the pilgrims who desired to enter the holy city were unmolested. This matter was settled in 1192.

On his return Richard was compelled to go *incog.* through Germany, as the authorities were opposed to him. He was discovered and confined till a large ransom was paid.

Philip and John, the king's brother, decided that Richard's extremity was their opportunity, and so concluded to divide up his kingdom between them. At this dramatic moment Richard, having paid his sixty thousand pounds ransom and tipped his custodian, entered the English arena, and the jig was up. John was obliged to ask pardon, and Richard generously gave it, with the exclamation, "Oh, that I could forget his injuries as soon as he will my forgiveness!"

[Illustration: RICHARD TRAVELLING INCOG. THROUGH GERMANY.]

Richard never secured a peace with Philip, but died, in 1199, from the effects of a wound received in France, and when but forty-two years of age. The longevity among monarchs of the present day is indeed gratifying when one reads of the brief lives of these old reigners, for it surely demonstrates that royalty, when not carried to excess, is rather conducive to health than otherwise.

Richard died from the effects of an arrow wound, and all his foes in this engagement were hanged, except the young warrior who had given him his death wound. Doubtless this was done to encourage good marksmanship.

England got no benefit from Richard's great daring and expensive picnics in Palestine; but of course he advertised Great Britain, and frightened foreign powers considerably. The taxation necessary to maintain an army in the Holy Land, where board was high, kept England poor; but every one was proud of Richard, because he feared not the face of clay.

John, the disagreeable brother, succeeded Richard, and reigned seventeen years, though his nephew, Arthur, the son of Geoffrey, was the rightful heir. Philip, who kept himself in pocket-money by starting one-horse rebellions against England, joined with Arthur long enough to effect a treaty, in 1200, which kept him in groceries several years, when he again brought Prince Arthur forward; but this was disastrous, for the young prince was captured and cruelly assassinated by request of his affectionate uncle, King John.

To be a relative of the king in those good old days was generally fatal. Let us rejoice that times have so greatly improved, and that the wicked monarch has learned to seat himself gingerly upon his bomb-infested throne.

[Illustration: JOHN CAUSED ARTHUR TO BE CRUELLY MURDERED.]

CHAPTER XII.

MAGNA CHARTA INTRODUCED: SLIGHT DIFFICULTIES ENCOUNTERED IN OVERCOMING AN UNPOPULAR AND UNREASONABLE PREJUDICE.

Philip called the miserable monarch to account for the death of Arthur, and, as a result, John lost his French possessions. Hence the weak and wicked son of Henry Plantagenet, since called Lackland, ceased to be a tax-payer in France, and proved to a curious world that a court fool in his household was superfluous.

John now became mixed up in a fracas with the Roman pontiff, who would have been justified in giving him a Roman punch. Why he did not, no Roman knows.

On the death of the Archbishop of Canterbury in 1205, Stephen Langton was elected to the place, with a good salary and use of the rectory. John refused to confirm the appointment, whereat Innocent III., the pontiff, closed the churches and declared a general lock-out. People were denied Christian burial in 1208, and John was excommunicated in 1209.

Philip united with the Pope, and together they raised the temperature for John so that he yielded to the Roman pontiff, and in 1213 agreed to pay him a comfortable tribute. The French king attempted to conquer England, but was defeated in a great naval battle in the harbor of Damme. Philip afterwards admitted that the English were not conquered by a Damme site; but the Pope absolved him for two dollars.

[Illustration: KING JOHN SIGNS THE MAGNA CHARTA.]

It was now decided by the royal subjects that John should be still further restrained, as he had disgraced his nation and soiled his ermine. So the barons raised an army, took London, and at Runnymede, June 15, 1215, compelled John to sign the famous Magna

Charta, giving his subjects many additional rights to the use of the climate, and so forth, which they had not known before.

Among other things the right of trial by his peers was granted to the freeman; and so, out of the mental and moral chaos and general strabismus of royal justice, everlasting truth and human rights arose.

Scarcely was the ink dry on Magna Charta, and hardly had the king returned his tongue to its place after signing the instrument, when he began to organize an army of foreign soldiers, with which he laid waste with fire and sword the better part of "Merrie Englande."

But the barons called on Philip, the general salaried Peacemaker Plenipotentiary, who sent his son Louis with an army to overtake John and punish him severely. The king was overtaken by the tide and lost all his luggage, treasure, hat-box, dress-suit case, return ticket, annual address, shoot-guns, stab-knives, rolling stock, and catapults, together with a fine flock of battering-rams.

This loss brought on a fever, of which he died, in 1216 A.D., after eighteen years of reign and wind.

A good execrator could here pause a few weeks and do well.

History holds but few such characters as John, who was not successful even in crime. He may be regarded roughly as the royal poultice who brought matters to a head in England, and who, by means of his treachery, cowardice, and phenomenal villany, acted as a counter-irritant upon the malarial surface of the body politic.

After the death of John, the Earl of Pembroke, who was Marshal of England, caused Henry, the nine-year-old son of the late king, to be promptly crowned.

Pembroke was chosen protector, and so served till 1219, when he died, and was succeeded by Hubert de Burgh. Louis, with the French forces, had been defeated and driven back home, so peace followed.

Henry III. was a weak king, as is too well known, but was kind. He behaved well enough till about 1231, when he began to ill-treat de Burgh.

He became subservient to the French element and his wife's relatives from Provence (pronounced *Provongs*). He imported officials by the score, and Eleanor's family never released their hold upon the public teat night or day. They would cry bitterly if deprived of same even for a moment. This was about the year 1236.

[Illustration: THE PROMPT CORONATION OF THE NINE-YEAR-OLD KING HENRY.]

Besides this, and feeling that more hot water was necessary to keep up a ruddy glow, the king was held tightly beneath the thumb of the Pope. Thus Italy claimed and secured the fat official positions in the church. The pontiff gave Henry the crown of Sicily with a C.O.D. on it, which Henry could not raise without the assistance of Parliament. Parliament did not like this, and the barons called upon him one evening with concealed brass knuckles and things, and compelled him to once more comply with the regulations of Magna Charta, which promise he rigidly adhered to until the committee had turned the first corner outside the royal lawn.

[Illustration: THE BARONS COMPELLED HENRY III. TO PROMISE COMPLIANCE
WITH THE MAGNA CHARTA.]

Possessing peculiar gifts as a versatile liar and boneless coward, and being entirely free from the milk of human kindness or bowels of compassion, his remains were eagerly sought after and yearned for by scientists long before he decided to abandon them.

Again, in 1258, he was required to submit to the requests of the barons; but they required too much this time, and a civil war followed.

Simon de Montfort, Earl of Leicester, at the head of the rebellious barons, won a victory over the king in 1264, and took the monarch and his son Edward prisoners.

Leicester now ruled the kingdom, and not only called an extra session of Parliament, but in 1265 admitted representatives of the towns and boroughs, thereby instituting the House of Commons, where self-made men might sit on the small of the back with their hats on and cry "Hear! Hear!"

The House of Commons is regarded as the bulwark of civil and political liberty, and when under good police regulations is still a great boon.

Prince Edward escaped from jail and organized an army, which in 1265 defeated the rebels, and Leicester and his son were slain. The wicked soldiery wreaked their vengeance upon the body of the fallen man, for they took great pride in their prowess as wreakers; but in the hearts of the people Leicester was regarded as a martyr to their cause.

Henry III. was now securely seated once more upon his rather restless throne, and as Edward had been a good boy for some time, his father gave him permission to visit the Holy Land, in 1270, with Louis of France, who also wished to go to Jerusalem and take advantage of the low Jewish clothing market. In 1272 Henry died, during the absence of his son, after fifty-six years of vacillation and timidity. He was the kind of king who would sit up half of the night trying to decide which boot to pull off first, and then, with a deep-drawn sigh, go to bed with them on.

Edward, surnamed "Longshanks," having collected many antiques, and cut up a few also, returned and took charge of the throne. He found England prosperous and the Normans and Saxons now thoroughly united and homogeneous. Edward did not hurry home as some would have done, but sent word to have his father's funeral made as cheery as possible, and remained over a year in Italy and France. He was crowned in 1274. In a short time, however, he had trouble with the Welsh, and in 1282, in battle, the Welsh prince became somehow entangled with his own name so that he tripped and fell, and before he could recover his feet was slain.

[Illustration: LONGSHANKS RECEIVES TIDINGS OF HIS FATHER'S DEATH.]

Wales having been annexed to the crown, Edward's son was vested with its government, and the heir-apparent has ever since been called the Prince of Wales. It is a good position, but becomes irksome after fifty or sixty years, it is said.

[Illustration: CONQUEST OF WALES.]

CHAPTER XIII.

FURTHER DISAGREEMENTS RECORDED: ILLUSTRATING THE AMIABILITY OF THE JEW AND THE PERVERSITY OF THE SCOT.

In 1278 the Jews, to the number of two hundred and eighty, were hanged for having in their possession clipped coins. Shortly afterwards all the Jews in England were imprisoned. Whenever times were hard the Jews were imprisoned, and on one job lot alone twelve thousand pounds were realized in ransom. And still the Jews are not yet considered as among the redeemed. In 1290 they were all banished from the kingdom and their property seized by the crown. This seizure of real estate turned the attention of the Jews to the use of diamonds as an investment. For four hundred years the Jews were not permitted to return to England.

Scotch wars were kept up during the rest of Edward's reign; but in 1291, with great reluctance, Scotland submitted, and Baliol, whose trouble with Bruce had been settled in favor of the former, was placed upon the throne. But the king was overbearing to Baliol, insomuch that the Scotch joined with the Normans in war with England, which resulted, in 1293, in the destruction of the Norman navy.

Philip then subpoenaed Edward, as Duke of Guienne, to show cause why he should not pay damages for the loss of the navy, which could not be replaced for less than twenty pounds, and finally wheedled Edward out of the duchy.

Philip maintained a secret understanding with Baliol, however, and Edward called a parliament, founded upon the great principle that "what concerns all should be approved by all." This was in 1295; and on this declaration, so far as successful government is concerned, hang all the law and the profits.

The following year Edward marched into Scotland, where he captured Baliol and sent him to France, where he died, in boundless obscurity, in 1297. Baliol was succeeded by the brave William Wallace, who won a great battle at Stirling, but was afterwards defeated entirely at Falkirk, and in 1305 was executed in London by request.

But the Scotch called to their aid Robert Bruce, the grandson of Baliol's competitor, and he was solemnly crowned at the Abbey of Scone.

During a successful campaign against these people Edward fell sick, and died in 1307. He left orders for the Scottish war to be continued till that restless and courageous people were subdued.

[Illustration: THE FRENCH KING ENTERS INTO A SECRET ALLIANCE WITH
BALIOL.]

Edward was called the English Justinian; yet those acts for which he is most famous were reluctantly done because of the demands made by a determined people.

During his reign gunpowder was discovered by Roger Bacon, whereby Guy Fawkes was made possible. Without him England would still be a slumbering fog-bank upon the shores of Time.

[Illustration: ROGER BACON DISCOVERS GUNPOWDER.]

Young Edward was not much of a monarch. He forgot to fight the Scots, and soon Robert Bruce had won back the fortresses taken by the English, and Edward II., under the influence of an attractive trifler named Gaveston, dawdled away his days and frittered away his nights. Finally the nobles, who disliked Gaveston, captured him and put him in Warwick Castle, and in 1312 the royal favorite was horrified to find near him a large pool of blood, and on a further search discovered his own head lying in the gutter of the court. Turning sick at the gory sight, he buried his face in his handkerchief and expired.

The nobles were forgiven afterwards by the king, who now turned his attention to the victorious Scots.

Stirling Castle and the Fortress of Berwick alone remained to the English, and Robert Bruce was besieging the latter.

The English, numbering one hundred thousand, at Bannockburn fought against thirty thousand Scots. Bruce surprised the cavalry with deep pits, and before the English could recover from this, an approaching reinforcement for the Scotch was seen coming over the hill. This consisted of "supes," with banners and bagpipes; and though they were really teamsters in disguise, their hostile appearance and the depressing music of the bagpipes so shocked the English that they did not stop running until they reached Berwick. The king came around to Berwick from Dunbar by steamer, thus saving his life, and obtaining much-needed rest on board the boat.[A]

[Footnote A: Doubtless this is an error, so far as the steamer is concerned; but the statement can do no harm, and the historian cannot be positive in matters of this kind at all times, for the strain upon his memory is too great. The critic, too, should not be forgotten in a work of this kind. He must do something to support his family, or he will become disliked.—AUTHOR.]

Edward found himself now on the verge of open war with Ireland and Wales, and the population of the Isle of Wight and another person, whose name is not given, threatened to declare war. The English nobles, too, were insubordinate, and the king, who had fallen under the influence of a man named Spencer and his father, was required by the best society, headed by Lancaster, to exile both of these wicked advisers.

Afterwards the king attacked Lancaster with his army, and having captured him, had him executed in 1322.

[Illustration: UNFORTUNATE KING WAS TREATED WITH REVOLTING CRUELTY.]

The Spencers now returned, and the queen began to cut up strangely and create talk. She formed the acquaintance of Roger Mortimer, who consented to act as her paramour. They organized a scheme to throw off the Spencers and dethrone Edward the Thinkless, her husband, in 1325.

Any one who has tried to be king even for a few weeks under the above circumstances must agree with the historian that it is no moonlight frolic.

Edward fled to Wales, but in 1326 was requested to come home and remain in jail there, instead of causing a scandal by staying away and spending his money in Wales. He was confined in Kenilworth Castle, while his son was ostensibly king, though his wife and Mortimer really managed the kingdom and behaved in a scandalous way, Mortimer wearing the king's clothes, shaving with his razor, and winding the clock every night as though he owned the place.[A] This was in 1327.

[Footnote A: The clock may safely be omitted from the above account, as later information would indicate that this may be an error, though there is no doubt that Mortimer at this time wore out two suits of the king's pajamas.—Author.]

In September the poor king was put to death by co-respondent Mortimer in a painful and sickening manner, after having been most inhumanly treated in Berkeley Castle, whither he had been removed.

Thus ends the sad history of a monarch who might have succeeded in a minor position on a hen farm, but who made a beastly fluke in the king business.

The assurance of Mortimer in treating the king as he did is a blot upon the fair page of history in high life. Let us turn over a new leaf.

[Illustration: ON A HEN FARM.]

CHAPTER XIV.

IRRITABILITY OF THE FRENCH: INTERMINABLE DISSENSION, ASSISTED BY THE PLAGUE, CONTINUES REDUCING THE POPULATION.

It is a little odd, but it is true, that Edward III. was crowned at fourteen and married at fifteen years of age. Princes in those days were affianced as soon as they were weighed, and married before they got their eyes open, though even yet there are many people who do not get their eyes opened until after marriage. Edward married Philippa, daughter of the Count of Hainault, to whom he had been engaged while teething.

In 1328 Mortimer mixed up matters with the Scots, by which he relinquished his claim to Scotch homage. Being still the gentleman friend of Isabella, the regent, he had great influence. He assumed, on the ratification of the above treaty by Parliament, the title of Earl of March.

The young prince rose to the occasion, and directed several of his nobles to forcibly drag the Earl of March from the apartments of the guilty pair, and in 1330 he became the Earl of Double-Quick March—a sort of forced March—towards the gibbet, where he was last seen trying to stand on the English climate. The queen was kept in close confinement during the rest of her life, and the morning papers of that time contained nothing of a social nature regarding her doings.

[Illustration: IN 1330 MORTIMER BECAME THE EARL OF DOUBLE-QUICK MARCH.]

The Scots, under David Bruce, were defeated at Halidon Hill in
1333, and
Bruce fled to France. Thus again under a vassal of the English king,
Edward Baliol by name, the Scotch crooked the reluctant hinges of
the

knee.

Edward now claimed to be a more direct heir through Queen Isabella than Philip, the cousin of Charles IV., who occupied the throne, so he proceeded to vindicate himself against King Philip in the usual way. He destroyed the French fleet in 1340, defeated Philip, though with inferior numbers, at Crécy, and demonstrated for the first time that cannon could be used with injurious results on the enemy.

[Illustration: EDWARD DEMONSTRATED AT THE BATTLE OF CRÉCY THAT CANNON
COULD BE USED WITH VIGOROUS RESULTS.]

In 1346 the Black Prince, as Edward was called, on account of the color of the Russia iron used in making his mackintosh, may be said to have commenced his brilliant military career. He captured Calais,—the key to France,—and made it a flourishing English city and a market for wool, leather, tin, and lead. It so continued for two hundred years.

The Scotch considered this a good time to regain their independence, and David Bruce took charge of the enterprise, but was defeated at Neville's Cross, in 1346, and taken prisoner.

Philippa here distinguished herself during the absence of the king, by encouraging the troops and making a telling equestrian speech to them before the battle. After the capture of Bruce, too, she repaired to Calais, where she prevented the king's disgraceful execution of six respectable citizens who had been sent to surrender the city.

[Illustration: A CLOSE CALL FOR THE SIX CITIZENS OF CALAIS.]

During a truce between the English and French, England was visited by the Black Death, a plague that came from Asia and bade fair to depopulate the country. London lost fifty thousand people, and at times there were hardly enough people left to bury the dead or till the fields. This contagion occurred in 1349, and even attacked the domestic animals.

[Illustration: NO MONARCH OF SPIRIT CARES TO HAVE HIS THRONE PULLED FROM
UNDER HIM JUST AS HE IS ABOUT TO OCCUPY IT.]

John having succeeded Philip in France, in 1350 Edward made another effort to recover the French throne; but no monarch of spirit cares to have his throne pulled from beneath him just as he is about to occupy it, and so, when the Black Prince began to burn and plunder southern France, his father made a similar excursion from Calais, in 1355.

The next year the Black Prince sent twelve thousand men into the heart of France, where they met an army of sixty thousand, and the English general offered all his conquests cheerfully to John for the privilege of returning to England; but John overstepped himself by demanding an unconditional surrender, and a battle followed in which the French were whipped out of their boots and the king captured. We should learn from this to know when we have enough.

This battle was memorable because the English loss was mostly confined to the common soldiery, while among the French it was peculiarly fatal to the nobility. Two dukes, nineteen counts, five thousand men-at-arms, and eight thousand infantry were killed, and a bobtail flush royal was found to have been bagged as prisoners.

For four years John was a prisoner, but well treated. He was then allowed to resume his renovated throne; but failing to keep good his promises to the English, he came back to London by request, and died there in 1364.

The war continued under Charles, the new French monarch; and though Edward was an able and courteous foe, in 1370 he became so irritated because of the revolt of Limoges, notwithstanding his former kindness to its people, that he caused three thousand of her citizens to be put to the sword.

The Black Prince fought no more, but after six years of illness died, in 1376, with a good record for courage and statecraft. His father, the king, survived him only a year, expiring in the sixty-fifth year of his age, 1377.

English literature was encouraged during his reign, and John Wickliffe, Gower, Chaucer, and other men whose genius greatly outstripped their orthography were seen to flourish some.

[Illustration: A STRIKING ILLUSTRATION OF WAT TYLER'S CONTROVERSY WITH
THE TAX RECEIVER.]

Edward III. was succeeded by his grandson, Richard, and war with France was maintained, though Charles the Wise held his own, with the aid of the Scotch under Robert II., the first of the Stuarts.

A heavy war-tax was levied *per capita* at the rate of three groats on male and female above the age of fifteen, and those who know the value of a groat will admit that it was too much. A damsel named Tyler, daughter of Wat the Tyler, was so badly treated by the assessor that her father struck the officer dead with his hammer, in 1381, and placed himself at the head of a revolt, numbering one hundred thousand people, who collected on Blackheath. Jack Straw and Rev. John Ball also aided in the convention. The latter objected to the gentlemen on general principles, claiming that Adam was no gentleman, and that Eve had still less claim in that direction.[A]

[Footnote A: Rev. John Ball chose as a war-cry and transparency these words:

"When Adam delved and Eve span,
Where was then the gentleman?"

Those who have tried it in modern times say that to be a gentleman is no sinecure, and the well-bred author falls in with this sentiment, though still regarding it as a great boon.—HISTORIAN.]

In this outbreak, and during the same year, the rebels broke into the city of London, burned the palaces, plundered the warehouses, and killed off the gentlemen wherever an *alibi* could not be established, winding up with the murder of the Archbishop of Canterbury.

During a conference with Tyler, the king was so rudely addressed by Wat, that Walworth, mayor of London, struck the rebel with his sword, and others despatched him before he knew exactly Wat was Wat.

Richard, to quiet this storm, acceded to the rebel demands until he could get his forces together, when he ignored his promises in a right royal manner in the same year. One of these concessions was the abolition of slavery and the novel use of wages for farm work. By his failure to keep this promise, serfdom continued in England four hundred years afterwards.

Richard now became unpopular, and showed signs of worthlessness. He banished his cousin Henry, and dispossessed him of his estates. This, of course, irritated Henry, who entered England while the king was in Ireland, and his forces were soon joined by sixty thousand malecontents.

Poor Richard wandered away to Wales, where he was in constant danger of falling off, and after living on chestnuts knocked from the high trees by means of his sceptre, he returned disgusted and took up his quarters in the Tower, where he died of starvation in 1400.

Nothing can be more pathetic than the picture of a king crying for bread, yet willing to compromise on tarts. A friendless king sitting on the hard stone floor of the Tower, after years spent on board of an elastic throne with rockers under it, would move even the hardened historian to tears. (A brief intermission is here offered for unavailing tears.)

[Illustration: A FRIENDLESS KING SITTING ON THE HARD
STONE FLOOR OF THE
TOWER.]

CHAPTER XV.

MORE SANGUINARY TRIUMPHS: ONWARD MARCH OF CIVILIZATION GRAPHICALLY DELINEATED WITH THE HISTORIAN'S USUAL COMPLETENESS.

The Plantagenet period saw the establishment of the House of Commons, and cut off the power of the king to levy taxes without the consent of Parliament. It also exchanged the judicial rough-and-tumble on horseback for the trial by jury. Serfdom continued, and a good horse would bring more in market than a man.

Agriculture was still in its infancy, and the farmer refused to adopt a new and attractive plough because it did not permit the ploughman to walk near enough to his team, that he might twist the tail of the patient bullock.

The costumes of the period seem odd, as we look back upon them, for the men wore pointed shoes with toes tied to the girdle, and trousers and coat each of different colors: for instance, sometimes one sleeve was black and the other white, while the ladies wore tall hats, sometimes two feet high, and long trains. They also carried two swords in the girdle, doubtless to protect them from the nobility.

[Illustration: SLAVES WERE BOUGHT AND SOLD AT THE FAIRS.]

Each house of any size had a "pleasance," and the "herberie," or physic garden, which was the pioneer of the pie-plant bed, was connected with the monasteries.

[Illustration: ASTROLOGY WAS THE FAVORITE STUDY OF THOSE TIMES.]

Roger Bacon was thrown into prison for having too good an education. Scientists in those days always ran the risk of being surprised, and more than one discoverer wound up by discovering himself in jail.

Astrology was a favorite amusement, especially among the young people.

Henry IV., son of John of Gaunt, fourth son of Edward III., became king in 1399, though Edmund Mortimer, Earl of March, and great-grandson of Lionel, the third son of Edward III., was the rightful heir. This boy was detained in Windsor Castle by Henry's orders.

[Illustration: HENRY PROTECTS THE CHURCH FROM HERESY.]

Henry succeeded in catching a heretic, in 1401, and burned him at the stake. This was the first person put to death in England for his religious belief, and the occasion was the origin of the epitaph, "Well done, good and faithful servant."

Conspiracies were quite common in those days, one of them being organized by Harry Percy, called "Hotspur" because of his irritability.
The ballad of Chevy Chase was founded upon his exploits at the battle of
Otterburn, in 1388. The Percys favored Mortimer, and so united with the
Welsh and Scots.

A large fight occurred at Shrewsbury in 1403. The rebels were defeated and Percy slain. Northumberland was pardoned, and tried it again, assisted by the Archbishop of York, two years later. The archbishop was executed in 1405. Northumberland made another effort, but was defeated and slain.

In 1413 Henry died, leaving behind him the record of a fraudulent sovereign who was parsimonious, sour, and superstitious, without virtue or religion.

He was succeeded by his successor, which was customary at that time. Henry V. was his son, a youth who was wild and reckless. He had been in jail for insulting the chief-justice, as a result of a drunken frolic and fine. He was real wild and bad, and had no more respect for his ancestry than a chicken born in an incubator. Yet he reformed on taking the throne.

[Illustration: HENRY V. HAD ON ONE OCCASION BEEN COMMITTED TO PRISON.]

Henry now went over to France with a view to securing the throne, but did not get it, as it was occupied at the time. So he returned; but at Agincourt was surprised by the French army, four times as large as his own, and with a loss of forty only, he slew ten thousand of the French and captured fourteen thousand. What the French were doing while this slaughter was going on the modern historian has great difficulty in figuring out. This battle occurred in 1415, and two years after Henry returned to France, hoping to do equally well. He made a treaty at Troyes with the celebrated idiot Charles VI., and promised to marry his daughter Catherine, who was to succeed Charles upon his death, and try to do better. Henry became Regent of France by this ruse, but died in 1422, and left his son Henry, less than a year old. The king's death was a sad blow to England, for he was an improvement on the general run of kings. Henry V. left a brother, the Duke of Bedford, who became Protector and Regent of France; but when Charles the Imbecile died, his son, Charles VII., rose to the occasion, and a war of some years began. After some time, Bedford invaded southern France and besieged Orléans.

[Illustration: HENRY, PROCLAIMED REGENT OF FRANCE, ENTERED PARIS IN
TRIUMPH.]

Joan of Arc had been told of a prophecy to the effect that France could only be delivered from the English by a virgin, and so she, though only a peasant girl, yet full of a strange, eager heroism which was almost inspiration, applied to the king for a commission.

[Illustration: JOAN OF ARC INDUCES THE KING TO BELIEVE THE TRUTH OF HER
MISSION.]

Inspired by her perfect faith and godlike heroism, the French fought like tigers, and, in 1429, the besiegers went home. She induced the king to be crowned in due form at Rheims, and asked for an honorable discharge; but she was detained, and the English, who afterwards captured her, burned her to death at Rouen, in 1431, on the charge of sorcery. Those who did this afterwards regretted it and felt mortified. Her death did the invaders no good; but above her ashes, and moistened by her tears,—if such a feat were possible,—liberty arose once more, and, in 1437, Charles was permitted to enter Paris and enjoy the town for the first time in twenty years. In 1444 a truce of six years was established.

Henry was a disappointment, and, as Bedford was dead, the Duke of Gloucester, the king's uncle, and Cardinal Beaufort, his guardian, had, up to his majority, been the powers behind the throne.

Henry married Margaret of Anjou, a very beautiful and able lady, who possessed the qualities so lacking in the king. They were married in 1445, and, if living, this would be the four hundred and fifty-first anniversary of their wedding. It is, anyway. (1896.)

The provinces of Maine and Anjou were given by the king in return for Margaret. Henry continued to show more and more signs of fatty degeneration of the cerebrator, and Gloucester, who had opposed the marriage, was found dead in his prison bed, whither he had been sent at Margaret's request. The Duke of York, the queen's favorite, succeeded him, and Somerset, another favorite, succeeded York. In 1451 it was found that the English had lost all their French possessions except Calais.

Things went from bad to worse, and, in 1450, Jack Cade headed an outbreak; but he was slain, and the king showing renewed signs of intellectual fag, Richard, Duke of York, was talked of as the people's choice on account of his descent from Edward III. He was for a few days Protector, but the queen was too strongly opposed to him, and he resigned.

[Illustration: RICHARD AND HIS ADHERENTS RAISING AN ARMY FOR THE REDRESS
OF GRIEVANCES.]

He then raised an army, and in a battle at St. Albans, in 1455, defeated the royalists, capturing the king. This was the opening of the War of the Roses,—so called because as badges the Lancastrians wore a red rose and the Yorkists a white rose. This war lasted over thirty years, and killed off the nobility like sheep. They were, it is said, virtually annihilated, and thus a better class of nobility was substituted.

The king was restored; but in 1460 there occurred the battle of Northampton, in which he was defeated and again taken prisoner by the
Earl of Warwick.

[Illustration: BY REQUEST OF MARGARET, HIS HEAD WAS RE-MOVED FROM HIS
BODY TO THE GATES OF YORK.]

Margaret was a woman of great spirit, and when the Duke of York was given the throne she went to Scotland, and in the battle of Wakefield her army defeated and captured the duke. At her request he was beheaded, and his head, ornamented with a paper crown, placed on the gates of York, as shown in the rather life-like—or death-like—etching on the preceding page.

The queen was for a time successful, and her army earned a slight reputation for cruelty also; but Edward, son of the late Duke of York, embittered somewhat by the flippant death of his father, was soon victorious over the Lancastrians, and, in 1461, was crowned King of England at a good salary, with the use of a large palace and a good well of water and barn.

CHAPTER XVI.

UNPLEASANT CAPRICES OF ROYALTY: INTRODUCTION OF PRINTING AS A SUBSIDIARY AID IN THE PROGRESS OF EMANCIPATION.

Henry VI. left no royal record worth remembering save the establishment of Eton and King's Colleges. Edward IV., who began his reign in 1461, was bold and active. Queen Margaret's army of sixty thousand men which attacked him was defeated and half her forces slaughtered, no quarter being given.

His title was now confirmed, and Margaret fled to Scotland. Three years later she attempted again to secure the throne through the aid of Louis XI., but failed. Henry, who had been in concealment, was now confined in the Tower, as shown in the engraving on the following page.

[Illustration: HENRY VI. IMPRESSED IN THE TOWER.]

Edward's marriage was not satisfactory, and, as he bestowed all the offices on his wife's relatives, Warwick deserted him and espoused the cause of Queen Margaret.

He had no trouble in raising an army and compelling Edward to flee. Henry was taken from the Tower and crowned, his rights having been recognized by Parliament. Warwick and his son-in-law, the Duke of Clarence, brother to Edward IV., were made regents, therefore, in 1471. Before the year was out, however, the tables were again turned, and Henry found himself once more in his old quarters in the Tower. Warwick was soon defeated and slain, and on the same day Margaret and her son Edward landed in England. She and Edward were defeated and taken prisoners at Tewkesbury, and the young prince cruelly put to death by the Dukes of Clarence and Gloucester, brothers of Edward IV. Margaret was placed in the Tower, and a day or two after Henry died mysteriously there, it is presumed at the hands of Gloucester, who was socially an unpleasant man to meet after dark.

Margaret died in France, in 1482, and the Lancastrians gave up all hope. Edward, feeling again secure, at the instigation of his younger brother, Richard, Duke of Gloucester, caused Clarence, the other brother, to be put to death, and then began to give his entire attention to vice, never allowing his reign to get into his rum or interfere with it.

He was a very handsome man, but died, in 1483, of what the historian calls a distemper. Some say he died of heart-failure while sleeping off an attack of coma. Anyway, he turned up his comatose, as one might say, and passed on from a spirituous life to a spiritual one, such as it may be. He was a counterfeit sovereign.

In 1474 the first book was printed in England, and more attention was then paid to spelling. William Caxton printed this book,—a work on chess. The form of the types came from Germany, and was used till James I. introduced the Roman type. James I. took a great interest in plain and ornamental job printing, and while trying to pick a calling card out of the jaws of a crude job-press in the early years of his reign, contributed a royal thumb to this restless emblem of progress and civilization. (See next page.)

[Illustration: JAMES I. CONTRIBUTING HIS MITE TO THE ADVANCEMENT OF
KNOWLEDGE.]

The War of the Roses having destroyed the nobility, times greatly improved, and Industry was declared constitutional.

Edward V. at twelve years of age became king, and his uncle Dick, Duke of Gloucester, became Protector. As such he was a disgrace, for he protected nobody but himself. The young king and his brother, the Duke of York, were placed in the Tower, and their uncle, Lord Hastings, and several other offensive partisans, on the charge of treason, were executed in 1483. He then made arrangements that he should be urged to accept the throne, and with a coy and reluctant grace peculiar to this gifted assassin, he caused himself to be proclaimed Richard III.

[Illustration: DEATH OF BUCKINGHAM.]

Richard then caused the young princes to be smothered in their beds, in what is now called the Bloody Tower. The Duke of Buckingham was at first loaded with honors in return for his gory assistance; but even he became disgusted with the wicked usurper, and headed a Welsh rebellion. He was not successful, and, in 1483, he received a slight testimonial from the king, as portrayed by the gifted artist of this work. The surprise and sorrow shown on the face of the duke, together with his thrift and economy in keeping his cigar from being spattered, and his determination that, although he might be put out, the cigar should not be, prove him to have been a man of great force of character for a duke.

Richard now espoused his niece, daughter of Edward IV., and in order to make the home nest perfectly free from social erosion, he caused his consort, Anne, to be poisoned. Those who believed the climate around the throne to be bracing and healthful had a chance to change their views in a land where pea-soup fog can never enter. Anne was the widow of Edward, whom Richard slew at Tewkesbury.

[Illustration: STONE COFFIN OF RICHARD III.]

Every one felt that Richard was a disgrace to the country, and Henry,
Earl of Richmond, succeeded in defeating and slaying the usurper on
Bosworth Field, in 1485, when Henry was crowned on the battlefield.

Richard was buried at Leicester; but during the reign of Henry VIII., when the monasteries were destroyed, Richard's body was exhumed and his stone coffin used for many years in that town as a horse-trough.

Shakespeare and the historians give an unpleasant impression regarding Richard's personality; but this was done in the interests of the Tudors, perhaps. He was highly intelligent, and if he had given less attention to usurpation, would have been more popular.

Under the administrations of the houses of Lancaster and York serfdom was abolished, as the slaves who were armed during the War of the Roses would not submit again to slavery after they had fought for their country.

Agriculture suffered, and some of the poor had to subsist upon acorns and wild roots. During those days Whittington was thrice Lord Mayor of London, though at first only a poor boy. Even in the land of lineage this poor lad, with a cat and no other means of subsistence, won his way to fame and fortune.

The manufacture of wool encouraged the growing of sheep, and, in 1455, silk began to attract attention.

During his reign Richard had known what it was to need money, and the rich merchants and pawnbrokers were familiar with his countenance when he came after office hours to negotiate a small loan.

[Illustration: RICHARD HAS A CONFERENCE WITH THE MONEY-LENDER.]

Science spent a great deal of surplus energy experimenting on alchemy, and the Philosopher's Stone, as well as the Elixir of Life, attracted much attention; but, as neither of these commodities are now on the market, it is presumed that they were never successful.

Printing may be regarded as the most valuable discovery during those bloody years, showing that Peace hath her victories no less than War, and from this art came the most powerful and implacable enemy to Ignorance and its attendant crimes that Progress can call its own.

No two authors spelled alike at that time, however, and the literature of the day was characterized by the most startling originality along that line.

The drama began to bud, and the chief rôles were taken by the clergy. They acted Bible scenes interspersed with local witticisms, and often turned away money.

Afterwards followed what were called Moral Plays, in which the bad man always suffered intensely on a small salary.

The feudal castles disappeared, and new and more airy architecture succeeded them. A better class of furniture also followed; but it was very thinly scattered through the rooms, and a person on rising from his bed in the night would have some difficulty in falling over anything. Tidies on the chairs were unknown, and there was only tapestry enough to get along with in a sort of hand-to-mouth way.

CHAPTER XVII.

BIOGRAPHY OF RICHARD III.: BEING AN ALLEGORICAL PANEGYRIC OF THE INCONTROVERTIBLE MACHINATIONS OF AN EGOTISTICAL USURPER.

[Illustration: RICHARD III.]

We will now write out a few personal recollections of Richard III. This great monarch, of whom so much has been said pro and con,—but mostly con,—was born at Fotheringhay Castle, October 2, 1452, in the presence of his parents and a physician whose name has at this moment escaped the treacherous memory of the historian.

Richard was the son of Richard, Duke of York, and Cecily Neville, daughter of the Earl of Westmoreland, his father being the legitimate heir to the throne by descent in the female line, so he was the head of the Yorkists in the War of the Roses.

Richard's father, the Duke of York, while struggling one day with Henry VI., the royal jackass that flourished in 1460, prior to the conquest of the Fool-Killer, had the misfortune, while trying to wrest the throne from Henry, to get himself amputated at the second joint. He was brought home in two pieces, and ceased to draw a salary as a duke from that on. This cast a gloom over Richard, and inspired in his breast a strong desire to cut off the heads of a few casual acquaintances.

He was but eight years of age at this time, and was taken prisoner and sent to Utrecht, Holland. He was returned in good order the following year. His elder brother Edward having become king, under the title of Edward IV., Richard was then made Duke of Gloucester, Lord High Admiral, Knight of the Garter, and Earl of Balmoral.

It was at this time that he made the celebrated *bon-mot* relative to dogs as pets.

Having been out the evening before attending a watermelon recital in the country, and having contributed a portion of his clothing to a barbed-wire fence and the balance to an open-faced Waterbury bull-dog, some one asked him what he thought of the dog as a pet.

Richard drew himself up to his full height, and said that, as a rule, he favored the dog as a pet, but that the man who got too intimate with the common low-browed bull-dog of the fifteenth century would find that it must certainly hurt him in the end.

[Illustration: THE MAN WHO GOT TOO INTIMATE WITH THE COMMON LOW-BROWED
BULL-DOG.]

He resided for several years under the tutelage of the Earl of Warwick, who was called the "Kingmaker," and afterwards, in 1470, fled to Flanders, remaining fled for some time. He commanded the van of the Yorkist army at the battle of Barnet, April 14, 1471, and Tewkesbury, May 4, fighting gallantly at both places on both sides, it is said, and admitting it in an article which he wrote for an English magazine.

He has been accused of having murdered Prince Edward after the battle, and also his father, Henry VI., in the Tower a few days later, but it is not known to be a fact.

Richard was attainted and outlawed by Parliament at one time; but he was careful about what he ate, and didn't get his feet wet, so, at last, having a good preamble and constitution, he pulled through.

He married his own cousin, Anne Neville, who made a first-rate queen. She got so that it was no trouble at all for her to reign while Dick was away attending to his large slaughtering interests.

Richard at this time was made Lord High Constable and Keeper of the
Pound. He was also Justiciary of North Wales, Seneschal of the Duchy of
Lancaster, and Chief of Police on the North Side.

His brother Clarence was successfully executed for treason in February, 1478, and Richard, without a moment's hesitation, came to the front and inherited the estates.

[Illustration: RICHARD HAD A STORMY TIME.]

Richard had a stormy time of it up to 1481, when he was made "protector and defender of the realm" early in May. He then proceeded with a few neglected executions. This list was headed—or rather beheaded—by Lord Chamberlain Hastings, who tendered his resignation in a pail of saw-dust soon after Richard became "protector and defender of the realm." Richard laid claim to the throne in June, on the grounds of the illegitimacy of his nephews, and was crowned July 6. So was his queen. They sat on this throne for some time, and each had a sceptre with which to welt their subjects over the head and keep off the flies in summer. Richard could wield a sceptre longer and harder, it is said, than any other middle-weight monarch known to history. The throne used by Richard is still in existence, and has an aperture in it containing some very old gin.

The reason this gin was left, it is said, was that he was suddenly called away from the throne and never lived to get back. No monarch should ever leave his throne in too much of a hurry.

Richard made himself very unpopular in 1485 by his forced loans, as they were called: a system of assessing a man after dark with a self-cocking writ and what was known as the headache-stick, a small weapon which was worn up the sleeve during the day, and which was worn behind the ear by the loyal subject after nightfall. It was a common sight, so says the historian, to hear the nightfall and the headache-stick fall at the same time.

[Illustration: THEY SAT ON THE THRONE FOR SOME TIME.]

The queen died in 1485, and Richard thought some of marrying again; but it got into the newspapers because he thought of it while a correspondent was going by, who heard it and telegraphed his paper who the lady was and all about it. This scared Richard out, and he changed his mind about marrying, concluding, as a mild substitute, to go into battle at Bosworth and get killed all at once. He did so on the 22d of August.

[Illustration: A MILD SUBSTITUTE FOR SECOND MARRIAGE.]

After his death it was found that he had rolled up his pantaloons above his knees, so that he would not get gore on them. This custom was afterwards generally adopted in England.

He was buried by the nuns of Leicester in their chapel, Richmond then succeeding him as king. He was buried in the usual manner, and a large amount of obloquy heaped on him.

That is one advantage of being great. After one's grave is filled up, one can have a large three-cornered chunk of obloquy put on the top of it to mark the spot and keep medical students away of nights.

Greatness certainly has its drawbacks, as the Duchess of Bloomer once said to the author, after she had been sitting on a dry-goods box with a nail in it, and had, therefore, called forth adverse criticism. An unknown man might have sat on that same dry-goods box and hung on the same nail till he was black in the face without causing remarks, but with the Duchess of Bloomer it was different,—oh, so different!

[Illustration: TOMB OF RICHARD III.]

CHAPTER XVIII.

DISORDER STILL THE POPULAR FAD: GENERAL ADMIXTURE OF PRETENDERS, RELIGION, POLITICS, AND DISGRUNTLED MONARCHS.

As a result of the Bosworth victory, Henry Tudor obtained the use of the throne from 1485 to 1509. He saw at once by means of an eagle eye that with the house of York so popular among his people, nothing but a firm hand and eternal vigilance could maintain his sovereignty. He kept the young Earl of Warwick, son of the Duke of Clarence, carefully indoors with massive iron gewgaws attached to his legs, thus teaching him to be backward about mingling in the false joys of society.

Henry Tudor is known to history as Henry VII., and caused some adverse criticism by delaying his nuptials with the Princess Elizabeth, daughter of Edward IV.

A pleasing practical joke at this time came near plunging the country into a bloody war. A rumor having gone forth that the Earl of Warwick had escaped from the Tower, a priest named Simon instructed a good-looking young man-about-town named Lambert Simnel to play the part, landed him in Ireland, and proceeded to call for troops. Strange to say, in those days almost any pretender with courage stood a good chance of winning renown or a hospitable grave in this way. But Lambert was not made of the material generally used in the construction of great men, and, though he secured quite an army, and the aid of the Earl of Lincoln and many veteran troops, the first battle closed the comedy, and the bogus sovereign, too contemptible even to occupy the valuable time of the hangman, became a scullion in the royal kitchen, while Simon was imprisoned.

[Illustration: SIMON, A PRIEST OF OXFORD, TAKES LAMBERT THE PRETENDER TO

For five years things were again dull, but at the end of that period an understudy for Richard, Duke of York, arose and made pretensions. His name was Perkin Warbeck, and though the son of a Flemish merchant, he was a great favorite at social functions and straw rides. He went to Ireland, where anything in the way of a riot was even then hailed with delight, and soon the York family and others who cursed the reigning dynasty flocked to his standard.

France endorsed him temporarily until Charles became reconciled to Henry, and then he dropped Perkin like a heated potato. Perk, however, had been well entertained in Paris as the coming English king, and while there was not permitted to pay for a thing. He now visited the Duchess of Burgundy, sister of Edward IV., and made a hit at once. She gave him the title of The White Rose of England (1493), and he was pleased to find himself so popular when he might have been measuring molasses in the obscurity of his father's store.

Henry now felt quite mortified that he could not produce the evidence of the murder of the two sons of Edward IV., so as to settle this gay young pretender; but he did not succeed in finding the remains, though they were afterwards discovered under the staircase of the White Tower, and buried in Westminster Abbey, where the floor is now paved with epitaphs, and where economy and grief are better combined, perhaps, than elsewhere in the world, the floor and tombstone being happily united, thus, as it were, killing two birds with one stone.

But how sad it is to-day to contemplate the situation occupied by Henry, forced thus to rummage the kingdom for the dust of two murdered princes, that he might, by unearthing a most wicked crime, prevent the success of a young pretender, and yet fearing to do so lest he might call the attention of the police to the royal record of homicide, regicide, fratricide, and germicide!

Most cruel of all this sad history, perhaps, was the execution of Stanley, the king's best friend in the past, who had saved his life in battle and crowned him at Bosworth. In an unguarded moment he had said that were he sure the young man was as he claimed, King

Edward's son, he—Stanley—would not fight against him. For this purely unpartisan remark he yielded up his noble life in 1495.

Warbeck for some time went about trying to organize cheap insurrections, with poor success until he reached Scotland, where James IV. endorsed him, and told him to have his luggage sent up to the castle. James also presented his sister Catherine as a spouse to the giddy young scion of the Flemish calico counter. James also assisted Perkin, his new brother-in-law, in an invasion of England, which failed, after which the pretender gave himself up. He was hanged amid great applause at Tyburn, and the Earl of Warwick, with whom he had planned to escape, was beheaded at Tower Hill. Thus, in 1499, perished the last of the Plantagenets of the male kind.

Henry hated war, not because of its cruelty and horrors, but because it was expensive. He was one of the most parsimonious of kings, and often averted war in order to prevent the wear and tear on the cannon. He managed to acquire two million pounds sterling from the reluctant tax-payer, yet no monarch ever received such a universal consent when he desired to pass away. If any regret was felt anywhere, it was so deftly concealed that his death, to all appearance, gave general and complete satisfaction.

[Illustration: A RELUCTANT TAX-PAYER.]

After a reign of twenty-four years he was succeeded by his second son,
Henry, in 1509, the elder son, Arthur, having died previously.

It was during the reign of Henry VII. that John and Sebastian Cabot were fitted out and discovered North America in 1497, which paved the way for the subsequent depopulation of Africa, Italy, and Ireland. South America had been discovered the year before by Columbus. Henry VII. was also the father of the English navy.

The accession of Henry VIII. was now hailed with great rejoicing. He was but eighteen years of age, but handsome and smart. He soon married Catherine of Aragon, the widow of his brother Arthur. She was six years his senior, and he had been betrothed to her under duress at his eleventh year.

A very fine snap-shot reproduction of Henry VIII. and Catherine in holiday attire, from an old daguerreotype in the author's possession, will be found upon the following page.

[Illustration: HENRY VIII. AND CATHERINE.]

Henry VIII. ordered his father's old lawyers, Empson and Dudley, tried and executed for being too diligent in business. He sent an army to recover the lost English possessions in France, but in this was unsuccessful. He then determined to organize a larger force, and so he sent to Calais fifty thousand men, where they were joined by Maximilian. In the battle which soon followed with the French cavalry, they lost their habitual *sang-froid* and most of their hand-baggage in a wild and impetuous flight. It is still called the Battle of the Spurs. This was in 1513.

In the report of the engagement sent to the king, nothing was said of the German emperor for the reason, as was said by the commander, "that he does not desire notice, and, in fact, Maximilian objections to the use of his name." This remark still furnishes food for thought on rainy days at Balmoral, and makes the leaden hours go gayly by.

During the year 1513 the Scots invaded England under James, but though their numbers were superior, they were sadly defeated at Flodden Field, and when the battle was over their king and the flower of their nobility lay dead upon the scene.

[Illustration: WOLSEY OUTSHINES THE KING.]

Wolsey, who was made cardinal in 1515 by the Pope, held a tremendous influence over the young king, and indirectly ruled the country. He ostensibly presented a humble demeanor, but in his innermost soul he was the haughtiest human being that ever concealed beneath the cloak of humility an inflexible, tough, and durable heart.

On the death of Maximilian, Henry had some notion of preëmpting the vacant throne, but soon discovered that Charles V. of Spain had a prior lien to the same, and thus, in 1520, this new potentate became the greatest power in the civilized world. It is hard to believe in the nineteenth or twentieth century that Spain ever had any influence with anybody of sound mind, but such the veracious historian tells us was once the case.

Francis, the French king, was so grieved and mortified over the success of his Spanish rival that he turned to Henry for comfort, and at Calais the two disgruntled monarchs spent a fortnight jousting, tourneying, in-falling, out-falling, merry-making, swashbuckling, and general acute gastritis.

[Illustration: THE FIELD OF THE CLOTH OF GOLD.]

It was a magnificent meeting, however, Wolsey acting as costumer, and was called "The Field of the Cloth of Gold." Large, portly men with whiskers wore purple velvet opera-cloaks trimmed with fur, and Gainsborough hats with ostrich feathers worth four pounds apiece (sterling). These corpulent warriors, who at Calais shortly before had run till overtaken by nervous prostration and general debility, now wore more millinery and breastpins and slashed velvet and satin facings and tinsel than the most successful and highly painted and decorated courtesans of that period.

The treaty here made with so much pyrotechnical display and *éclat* and hand-embroidery was soon broken, Charles having caught the ear of Wolsey with a promise of the papal throne upon the death of Leo X., which event he joyfully anticipated.

Henry, in 1521, scored a triumph and earned the title of Defender of the Faith by writing a defence of Catholicism in answer to an article written by Martin Luther attacking it. Leo died soon after, and, much to the chagrin of Wolsey, was succeeded by Adrian VI.

[Illustration: HENRY WRITES A TREATISE IN DEFENCE OF THE
CATHOLIC
CHURCH.]

War was now waged with France by the new alliance of Spain and England; but success waited not upon the English arms, while, worse than all, the king was greatly embarrassed for want of more scudii. Nothing can be more pitiful, perhaps, than a shabby king waiting till all his retainers have gone away before he dare leave the throne, fearing that his threadbare retreat may not be protected. Henry tried to wring something from Parliament, but without success, even aided by that practical apostle of external piety and internal intrigue, Wolsey. The latter, too, had a second bitter disappointment in the election of Clement VII. to succeed Adrian, and as this was easily traced to the chicanery of the emperor, who had twice promised the portfolio of pontiff to Wolsey, the latter determined to work up another union between Henry and France in 1523.

War, however, continued for some time with Francis, till, in 1525, he was defeated and taken prisoner. This gave Henry a chance to figure with the queen regent, the mother of Francis, and a pleasant treaty was made in 1526. The Pope, too, having been captured by the emperor, Henry and Francis agreed to release and restore him or perish on the spot. Quite a well-written and beguiling account of this alliance, together with the Anne Boleyn affair, will be found in the succeeding chapter.

[Illustration: CHARLES II. CONCEALED IN THE "ROYAL OAK," WHILE HIS
PURSUERS PASSED UNDER HIM (1651).]

[Illustration: OLIVER CROMWELL IN DISSOLVING PARLIAMENT SEIZED THE MACE,
EXCLAIMING, "TAKE AWAY THIS BAUBLE!" (1653).]

[Illustration: A BOOK ENTITLED "KILLING NO MURDER", BOLDLY ADVISING THE
REMOVAL OF THE USURPER, CAUSED CROMWELL CEASELESS ANXIETY (1658).]

[Illustration: HENRY VIII. PLUNDERING THE CHURCHES AND MONASTERIES OF
THEIR POSSESSIONS.]

[Illustration: AFTER THE DEATH OF JANE SEYMOUR, HENRY VIII. TURNED HIS
ATTENTION TO THE SELECTION OF A NEW QUEEN, DECIDING ON ANNE OF CLEVES, A

PROTESTANT PRINCESS WITH WHOSE PORTRAIT HE HAD BEEN HIGHLY PLEASED. THE
ORIGINAL SO GREATLY DISAPPOINTED HIM THAT HE SOON DIVORCED HER.]

[Illustration: EDWARD VI., SUCCESSOR TO HENRY VIII., AETAT. TEN YEARS,
WHOSE ATTENTION TO HIS STUDIES AND THE GENTLENESS OF HIS DISPOSITION
MADE HIM MUCH BELOVED (1547-53).]

[Illustration: THE GREAT INFLUX OF GOLD AND SILVER FROM THE NEW WORLD
CAUSED AN INCREASE IN THE PRICE OF COMMODITIES (1549).]

[Illustration: THE CHERISHED OBJECT OF MARY WAS TO RESTORE THE CATHOLIC RELIGION, AND HER CHIEF COUNSELLORS WERE BISHOPS GARDINER AND BONNER (1554).]

[Illustration: QUEEN ELIZABETH (1558-1603).]

[Illustration: SIR WALTER RALEIGH.]

[Illustration: QUEEN ELIZABETH SIGNING THE DEATH-WARRANT OF MARY QUEEN
OF SCOTS, 1587.]

[Illustration: DEATH OF QUEEN ELIZABETH, MARCH 24, 1603. FOR TEN DAYS
PREVIOUS TO HER DEATH SHE LAY UPON THE FLOOR SUPPORTED BY CUSHIONS.]

[Illustration: DISCOVERY OF THE GUNPOWDER PLOT (1605).]

[Illustration: EFFIGY OF GUY FAWKES.]

[Illustration: THE SCOTCH COULD NOT ENDURE ARCHBISHOP LAUD'S RITUALISTIC

PRACTICES, AND JENNY GEDDES THREW A STOOL AT HIS HEAD.]

[Illustration: SIR WALTER RALEIGH, AT HIS EXECUTION, ASKED TO EXAMINE
THE AXE. HE POISED IT, AND RUNNING HIS THUMB ALONG THE EDGE, SAID, WITH
A SMILE, "THIS IS SHARP MEDICINE," ETC. (1618).]

[Illustration: PRINCE CHARLES AND BUCKINGHAM TRAVEL TO SPAIN IN
DISGUISE, SO THAT THE FORMER MIGHT PAY HIS ADDRESSES IN PERSON TO THE
INFANTA.]

[Illustration: CHARLES I. FORCED TO GIVE HIS ASSENT TO THE "PETITION OF
EIGHTS" (1628).]

[Illustration: OLIVER CROMWELL.]

[Illustration: EARL OF STRAFFORD RECEIVING LAUD'S BLESSING ON THE WAY
TO EXECUTION (1641).]

[Illustration: SAMPLE PAGE OF ROUNDHEADS (1642).]